"I think there's a werewolf in Stagwater," Sylvie said.

The words had come out before she'd thought them through.

The foot or so of space between them crackled, tension mounting in the silence. Then Rand, shifting himself more comfortably, said, "There's no such thing as werewolves."

"You said the same thing about witches," she reminded him.

"And you whipped out your membership card and proved me wrong. What are you going to do now—turn into a wolf?"

"No. Are you?" The challenge hung between them. It wouldn't take much. His narrowed pale eyes already looked lupine, feral. When he smiled, his bared teeth completed the picture.

He loomed closer, and she drew back. "The idea has its merits," he growled. And in one motion, too fluid to be a lunge, he pressed her back against the door and covered her mouth with his own.

Evelyn Vaughn "once went with friends to see a psychic and she foretold our life's mission. Mine? 'To write.'"

That made sense, because she started her first book at the age of six and was first published at the age of twelve. Her love of writing was further enhanced by her large family, all of whom are avid readers. This compelled Evelyn to graduate with a master's degree in comparative literature. Now she finds herself on both sides of the business: teaching college-level literature and writing novels!

Although Evelyn still hasn't found Mr. Right, she is busily creating him in every book she writes.

WAITING FOR THE WOLF MOON

EVELYN VAUGHN

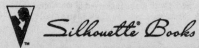
Silhouette® Books

Published by Silhouette Books

America's Publisher of Contemporary Romance

SILHOUETTE BOOKS

ISBN 0-373-51189-2

WAITING FOR THE WOLF MOON

Visit Silhouette at www.eHarlequin.com

Printed in U.S.A.

PROLOGUE

Wort Moon

From Mississippi and points east, the full moon rose into the Louisiana sky. The waters of the Gulf of Mexico and the Mississippi Delta captured her silver and scattered it in chuckling waves. Farther north, in a grove of cleared underbrush, in the woods north of Lake Pontchartrain, four women sat in pine-shadowed moonlight.

They had no altar, no candles, just a small campfire into which they took turns throwing bits of dried herbs. The wort incense filled the humid clearing as nature reclaimed a small portion of what she had yielded that year. A stalk of basil, a clump of marjoram, a large leaf of comfrey....

One woman, a slim brunette, paused, lost in thoughts of a previous moon and the death it had delivered. She tried to shudder the memory off; that was past. It hadn't been the moon's fault.

"You okay?" murmured the redhead beside her, her tone mixing genuine concern with hushed reverence.

"I'm fine." The brunette threw a sprig of mint into the crackling flame, resuming the ritual. But she wondered why she remembered now, after over a year.

Was there any such thing as coincidence?

And, farther east, under the moon, a young man—
Dennis Gareaux, from nearby Slidell—hiked along
the graveled edge of a two-lane blacktop road, his
attention focused more on the dry-tanked Chevette
he'd left a half mile behind him than on the celestial
display above him. It was too damn hot, and Denny
didn't have much interest in pretty nights.

Then he heard a whining in the woods.

He paused, intrigued—there had been trouble with
wild dogs earlier in the summer. A group of hunters
had gone into the swamp and killed them all off, but
he'd missed the fun. Maybe a few pups or loners had
survived.

The whining continued, hardly threatening. Denny
judged the width of the ditch that bordered the road.
Despite the algae over the water, even the ditch reflected the moon's silver.

All the easier to jump. Denny did, regained his
footing, and listened to the darkness beyond.

A whimper.

Underbrush knotted the close-set pines together;
prickly vines of wild blackberry wove through thicker
patches of honeysuckle, waist deep in some places,
deeper next to dying trees. But, hell, he was wearing
thick jeans. He waded his way out of the moonlight
and into the woods, wincing as blackberry thorns tore
into his hand. He hoped any local snakes could hear
him coming.

The whimpering stopped.

"Hey!" Denny whispered, crouching to retrieve a

thick branch from the needle-carpeted ground. Vines scratched at his hand again. "Hey, pooch." Crickets answered, and toads—what passed around here for silence.

"Hey, doggie!" Denny raised his rough voice, silencing some of the crickets. "Here, dog—"

A claw tore across his throat, turning his call into a hoarse scream. He heard a snarl he hadn't heard in almost twenty years of hunting. He fell, his weight yanking vines loose. Thorns bit his face and hands. His blood spattered brown pine needles before he landed on them. He tried to roll away, disoriented. A flash of fur—silver in the moonlight—caught his stunned attention. Then Denny felt teeth sinking into his shoulder, and he fainted.

And in the woods of Louisiana, a wolf raised its head to howl an unanswered call to its Lady Moon.

CHAPTER ONE

Waxing Moon

There was a hearse parked in front of her bookstore.

Waiting for an oncoming gravel truck to pass before turning left into the parking lot, Sylvie Peabody studied the vehicle. Long. Black. Shiny. Definitely a hearse. It even had red curtains—velvet?—with gold tassels.

She couldn't see the driver.

She wasn't sure she wanted to.

She hoped he was alone.

The gravel truck rumbled by, spattering pebbles against her scarred windshield, and she pulled up in front of her store. Chalky clamshells crunched beneath her tires as she braked the lemon-colored '79 Pinto, yanked on the parking brake and cut the engine. Some jobs offered excitement regularly. Her former career, as a reporter for an avant-garde weekly in Los Angeles, had been such a job—but she'd left it to open UnderCover. At the only bookstore in Stagwater, Louisiana, an exciting day was when a shipment from their wholesaler arrived.

Hearses registered way off the excitometer.

Sylvie slid her yellow scarf off her feathery brown hair and draped it on the parking brake for the open-windowed drive home, then selected a store key from her key ring. Most comfortable in observer mode, she casually glanced over at the vehicle several spaces down. It was empty. At least, the front end was.

Taking a deep breath, she tried to *sense* the hearse—or rather, to sense what self-defense teachers call an "uh-oh" feeling, which would be her cue to jam the Pinto into reverse and scatter clamshells.

She didn't feel anything, which was no surprise. Her instincts had stunk for some time now.

Oh, well. She rolled up the windows and climbed out of the Pinto. Maybe some funeral-home worker had stopped in at the Po-Boy next door for a sandwich before a pickup.

Or a delivery.

She paused, jiggling her keys in indecision.

Was it a delivery? It couldn't hurt to glance in the window, just to make sure there wasn't a casket in back. At least she would *know*.

The hearse, despite its shine, looked fairly old. It had fins on the back. Behind her own transparent reflection in the window, the curtains were indeed velvet. And beyond the curtains…

After glancing around self-consciously, she stepped forward and leaned closer to the long window.

"Boo!"

She flew back at the sudden appearance of a face opposite hers, replacing her own reflection. She was a parking space away, just beginning to breathe again, when the hearse's back door opened and the same face poked out. "Gotcha," it said with a wolfish grin.

Warily she watched him. She would wait until her pulse rate dropped a few notches from critical to answer.

The dark-haired "corpse" clambered out of the hearse and shut the door behind him, then wiped his hands on his jeans, very much alive. She certainly couldn't imagine someone being caught dead dressed in those baggy jeans, and sockless. His faded, short-sleeved shirt hung open against the heat to reveal a nice expanse of lean, tanned stomach and chest. She couldn't imagine a corpse with a ponytail, either, and this man wore his ebony hair pulled back from his animated face in a neat queue. His mischievous grin and laughing gray eyes made her suddenly consider him attractive.

Dangerously attractive.

She suspected she would regret asking, but… "What were you doing back there?"

"Me?" He leaned easily against a black fender. "Merely stretching out until the bookstore opens. There aren't that many options in the back of a hearse." He appeared completely serious.

She had to tear her eyes off him to walk away and unlock the door to UnderCover. She'd read somewhere that everyone you met you had somehow drawn to you. A meeting like this threw the concept into a whole new—and weird—perspective.

"Nice," said the man, following her into the air-conditioned coolness of the shop. She'd renovated a gutted hardware store to open UnderCover. Now only a tremendous sense of space marked its past incarnation. Each of the tall, glossy wooden shelves had symbols cut out of the sides—hearts in the romance section, stars in the fantasy aisle, and so on. It was one benefit of having a sister-in-law with a jig-saw…and ulterior motives for hanging around the shop. The signs labeling each area had been crafted by a local amateur artist.

"Take your time looking around," she said, raising the window blinds—the old-fashioned cloth kind, dyed yellow—and flipping the sign on the door over to read Open.

"Oh, I've got plenty," he answered airily.

Did he mean books? Studying the back of his head and his sleek, dark ponytail, she suspected he meant time.

She wasn't used to having someone in the store while she opened. As she stepped onto the dais hold-ing the counter area—"The better to see you with, my dear"—she had the unsettling sensation of being watched. She turned on the cash register, counted out her change three times before she got it to match the previous night's total, then finally gave in to discom-fort and looked back toward her customer.

He didn't *look* like the sort of person who would drive a hearse. Then again, he *was* crouched in front of the horror section.

"The latest Bill Westbrook novel just came out in paperback," she offered, picking a bestselling horror author.

He smiled. Such a dangerously charming smile. It

didn't fit his mode of transportation at all. "I've got it in hardcover. Good book."

She turned on the radio, flipped to a New Orleans New Age station and tried to relax to some perky dulcimer music. But the air felt charged, as it might before a storm.

He stood, wandered past the romance section, past Westerns, past Erotica. He paused and backed up for a second glance.

She studied her selection of jar candles—there was something homey about an open flame—and chose the pink one. When she lit it, a rosy scent drifted into the shop.

He dragged himself away from a shelf of Victorian romps, glanced at his watch and headed toward the back shelves.

She realized she was watching him too closely and turned her attention back to her work. As if she had dozens of unfinished tasks to choose from. A bookstore in small-town Louisiana wasn't exactly a busy place. No matter. It was a *necessary* place. She pulled some used books out from under her counter—they'd come in late the previous afternoon—and began sorting them into piles according to price. With a good deal of willpower she managed not to glance back at her intriguing customer for several minutes.

When she did, he was frowning at her display of books on magic and the occult, which was tucked in back, where only people who looked could find it. Uh-oh.

"Can I help you?"

He glanced her way. "I've been told I'm beyond help," he confessed solemnly. "But what do mothers know?" His gray eyes danced, and a dimple softened one cheek above his long, shadowed jaw.

Her lips twitched. "Are you looking for a certain book?"

"In fact..."

She recognized his pause. He was curious about a controversial subject, and worried that she'd be put off by it. She tried to look particularly nonthreatening.

"I'm trying to find some books about witches." Little did he know. Some of my best friends... "The town library doesn't have much on the subject," he added by way of explanation.

"No kidding?" She descended from the dais and went to join him. "You've come to the right place. We've got Cunningham—" She had to reach particularly close to him to angle out the books. It felt like reaching through a warm draft, or an electrical current.

Just her imagination—lousy instincts, remember? She crouched to angle out Starhawk, Valiente, Weinstein. He crouched beside her.

Disturbance. Warmth. What an odd, silvery color his eyes were, framed by dark, blunt lashes.

"Are there any spells in these?" he asked, sinking back on his haunches for balance.

"Some."

His eyes widened, and he looked normal again.

"Think of them as the concentrated power of positive thinking, channeling natural energy and personal power.'' She felt the uneasy need to qualify what she'd said. ''Assuming you believe in personal power.'' And if he didn't, what was he doing with so bloody much of it?

As he reached out to help her to her feet, his strong, callused fingers brushed the soft skin inside her elbow, and warm, tingling energy pulsed from him. She stepped back from the pleasant violation, unbalanced.

''Nothing like summoning demons?'' he asked softly. ''Hexes? Curses? Turning people into amphibious creatures of the four-legged persuasion?''

''Not in mass-market paperback,'' she whispered. Certainly not in anything *she* stocked.

''What about love spells?'' He leaned a little closer, his shirt falling open to show more of his hair-shadowed chest. The teasing intimacy of his voice both lulled and aroused her, like hypnotism, giving new meaning to the term *alpha male*.

''I think…'' That's right, *think*. Distance. ''There are some spells to draw love, but not to target a single person. That's considered manipulative.''

''Damn.'' His regretful shrug brought back reality. ''Could've come in handy.''

You could try Voudun. No, she was *not* going to give someone that kind of lead, no matter how pleasant the image of him casting a love spell was.

He crouched again and extracted one of the books she'd indicated for closer examination. She retreated to the safe distance of the counter and her pricing. She started using yellow stickers, then had to redo them with the blue ones that indicated used books.

A dreamlike synthesizer piece replaced the dulcimer music. Then he was in front of her, laying four of the books she'd recommended on the counter. Conscious of his eyes on her, she rang them up. The thought of him practicing magic—perhaps nude, the way some witches did—tickled her imagination. She firmly ignored it.

"Would you like a bag?"

"No—but the IRS may want the receipt."

She handed it to him before the connection clicked. Business expense.

And he drove a *hearse?*

Her reporter's curiosity kicked in. "What exactly do you do?"

He folded his bare, tanned arms on the counter and leaned across them. "In what context?" he asked huskily. He had a point. The possibilities were, in fact, endless.

"In a context the IRS would care about," she replied, careful to keep her tone casual, controlled. "Officially."

"Oh! That!"

"If you don't mind my asking?"

"Not at all." He glanced toward the shop's front windows, where she'd taped fliers for the community theater, an upcoming concert, a blood drive. "However…do you display ads for local businesses?"

Odd change of subject. "Depends on the business."

"Then why don't I surprise you? The copy shop is nearly open, and I've got an order to pick up." He winked at her. "I never underestimate the value of suspense." Heading toward the door, he paused and shifted his books.

"Not even any eye-of-newt, toe-of-frog stuff?" he asked plaintively, studying the paperbacks.

"Try Shakespeare. *Macbeth.*"

His last smile stayed with her long after the hearse had pulled out of the parking lot. There was something significant about him, something… She couldn't place it. Something to be wary of, though—especially since she responded so easily to whatever he had. Men with that much charm posed their own kind of danger.

She didn't need her old instincts to know that.

Not that everyone accepted her lack of instincts.

"Have you felt anything weird today?" asked her sister-in-law, Brigit, during their daily phone conversation. Pots clanked in the background for a moment, and then running water muffled the connection—Brie always called while she was fixing lunch. Sylvie had moved to Stagwater as much to be with Brie, her friend and mentor, as to be with her brother, Steve.

Did attraction to a complete stranger constitute weird? "Why do you ask?" On her end, Sylvie kept her voice low; she had a customer. Luckily Mrs. Foster, called Miss—Miz—Amanda in these parts, seemed to be lost in the mystery rack.

"I mean about the death!"

It took a moment for Sylvie, phone trapped between shoulder and cheek, to figure out what death

Brigit was referring to. "You mean the dog attack? That was over two weeks ago!"

"Exactly, and Steve says the FBI report is due any day now. You know something's weird when the New Orleans medical examiner wants a second opinion on his autopsy." Brie's voice dropped. "It worries me."

"It was a violent death, Brie." A publisher's catalog on her lap, Sylvie uncapped a felt pen with her teeth and circled an advertisement for a popular romance author. "Of course it worries you."

"And you? You could always read things—what do you feel about it?"

"I'm a psi potato now, remember?"

Miz Amanda looked toward her, evidently confused. Sylvie nodded casually and waved. Maybe she should just wear a T-shirt reading "I HEART Metaphysics."

Brigit said, as usual, "The feelings aren't what stopped, kiddo. You just stopped letting yourself feel them. And if you'd ditch your guilt about Eddie..."

"Yeah, yeah, I've heard it." It bothered Sylvie that the thought of Eddie, her year-dead fiancé, led to thoughts of this morning's stranger. Did men always have to come with trouble attached, or had Eddie just been an outstanding specimen in that way? "And you're one to talk guilt, Miss I-Hate-Lying-to-My-Husband." Brigit Peabody was as much a witch as anyone...when around other witches. But because her family tradition emphasized silence among outsiders, she refused to come out of the broom closet, even for Sylvie's brother.

"Silence is the secret of keeping secrets, kid. And some people still think witches should be burned."

But not everybody. Some people bought esoteric writings in paperback. People with silvery eyes and wolfish charm.

By now Miz Amanda was approaching the counter, arms loaded with secondhand mysteries. "I gotta go," admitted Sylvie, unwilling to juggle a mundane and an arcane conversation at the same time. "See you later."

"At dinner. 'Bye."

When Sylvie hung up the phone, Miz Amanda said, "I couldn't help overhearing."

Uh-oh, thought Sylvie, until the woman continued, "Were you discussing the Gareaux murder?"

"Murder?" repeated Sylvie conversationally, ringing up the purchase. "I thought it was a dog attack. You know how people from the city desert their dogs around here...." Miz Amanda's level gaze caught and held hers. *Yes, and autopsies for people killed by wild dogs always take weeks.*

"Not after the way the menfolk cleared out those woods when poor Mrs. Thomas died. Why, my Wade assured me that they'd gotten every wild dog out of there, and I believe him."

The rope of bells on the door jingled. The hunk in the hearse? No. Her friend, Mary Deveraux, waved a quick hello and drifted toward magic and the occult.

"I think the murderer was probably some outsider,

come up from the city to cause trouble.'' Miz Amanda nodded emphatically, clearly pleased with her own powers of deduction. "After all, they found the boy's body right near the highway, they did. The murderer only *wants* us to think it was dogs that did it." After fishing out her payment, she closed her change purse with a snap. "Or maybe it was a ritual killing—one of those demon-worshiping voodoo people from the bayou, like in the movies!''

Behind Miz Amanda, Mary Deveraux held up her hands as if they were claws. With her petite build and honey-colored hair, she hardly looked threatening, but Sylvie frowned anyway. Mary wore her pentagram—pointing up, not inverted—for anyone to see. Miz Amanda might actually take fright at the Wiccan symbol.

"There are fewer ritual murders than the movies would lead you to believe, Miz Amanda,'' Sylvie assured her, bagging the books. "And it's not voodoo people who commit them. I'm sure the police will find who or what killed Dennis Gareaux once they get the FBI report.''

Nodding emphatically, Miz Amanda left the store with a friendly tinkling of bells.

"Those demon-worshiping voodoo people,'' Mary said, mimicking Miz Amanda, as she came over to the counter. "They don't worship demons any more than I do.''

Sylvie grinned at her fervor, not about to get caught up in that topic. "So why aren't you at the Wellness Club?''

"I'm off for the day. A customer saw my penta-gram and freaked. Thought I was some kind of dia-bolical massage therapist. Heck, I don't even believe in devils, much less—"

"Yeah, yeah, you don't have to convince me that you're harmless. I've seen you capture and relocate roaches."

"Speaking of which, you want lunch?" Mary chuckled at the face Sylvie pulled. "I'll run next door to the Po-Boy. My treat, to show the Fates how little I care about losing a customer."

Sylvie agreed. But as soon as the shop was empty, her thoughts rushed back to this morning's mysterious customer—the one who hadn't returned. She went over to the Magic and the Occult shelves, wondering how seriously he took the subject. Her shop offered the best—perhaps the only—selection of metaphysi-cal books this side of the lake, so she often had New Age customers referred to her. But no, he'd asked questions no insider would have to ask. She drifted to the horror section where he'd first looked. Strong presence or not, he'd only been a customer. So why were images of laughing eyes, dimples and a ponytail haunting her? What made him important?

She laid her left hand on one of the books she'd seen him perusing. She felt...nothing. Of course. She was tired of feeling nothing.

The bells rang then, spoiling any slim chance of a psychic impression. "It's *that* stuff that causes the trouble, you know." With a broad sweep of the Po-Boy bag she held, Mary waved at the horror section.

"That and the TV shows and the movies Miss Amanda so kindly mentioned. You can talk midwives and goddess worship and 'harm none' until you're blue in the face, but as long as stories about wart-nosed, evil hags titillate the masses..."

"Mmm-hmm." Sylvie went back to her perch behind the counter and poked a straw into a cola.

The blonde hitched herself up onto the counter, making herself taller than Sylvie. "You aren't very sympathetic."

"I'm distracted," Sylvie admitted. "There was a hearse in front of the store this morning."

"I don't buy into negative omens."

"It wasn't one. There was a really good-looking guy in it, and he wanted books on—"

Mary's hazel eyes went round. "Was he dark?"

"You've seen him?" Maybe Mary knew who he was and why he drove a hearse.

"Not exactly—but I've *seen* him." The emphasis said it all. Mary was a precog, a psychic skilled at telling the future, and she read tarot. "You want to hear?"

Sylvie extracted her submarine sandwich. "The last time you predicted a man entering my life, it was Romeow," she pointed out dryly, as if her nerves hadn't just gone on full alert, and took a bite. "And he really is an alley cat—he left me for Brie."

"I'm more experienced now, and you should know what I *saw*." Mary's serious expression convinced Sylvie to nod. "The reading was definitely about you, Queen of Swords. But it was dominated by a dark-

haired man, creative and determined—I g⌣ ⌐ sense
of something occult-related, but he's more like a businessman than a practitioner. Heavy on the pentacles,
but with cups in the right places. Definite romance
possibility.'' Sylvie busied herself with her drink.
''But his past is shrouded in mystery, and possibly
violence. What's worse—so's his future.''

''Violent, or mysterious?''

''Both. He's hiding something, and it could cause
the possible relationship to blow up. We're talking
major arcana. The Tower.''

''But if it's major arcana, isn't it fated? Shouldn't
I avoid him completely?'' asked Sylvie, chewing
French bread and lettuce. One minute she didn't even
have a relationship, the next minute it was doomed.

''Not necessarily, not in the position it was in.''
Mary's voice took on the smooth distance it always
did during readings. ''Trouble's a definite possibility,
that's a fact. But you may be able to help him—at
great risk to yourself.''

''Physical or emotional risk? I mean, Eddie must
have immunized me to any further emo—''

Mary put down her own sandwich. ''Both, friend.
That's why I wanted to tell you about it. And since
you've got the instincts of a paperweight—''

''Thank you very much.''

Mary shrugged. ''So this guy was dark haired?''

Occult-related. Businessman, not practitioner. Oh,
my. ''Yeah. He drove a hearse, bought some books
on witches and kept the receipt for the IRS.''

Mary licked her finger and chalked one up on an

invisible scoreboard. "Can I call 'em, or what? So, are you going to see him again? 'Cause if you do, you want to go into it with both eyes open."

Sylvie took another bite of her sandwich, to postpone answering. "There is no 'it' to go into. I don't even know his name."

"But?" Damn, it was tough having a psychic for a friend.

"But he did kind of flirt with me…and he said he'd be back with a flier for my window. I guess I shouldn't encourage him." That would be better, anyway.

"I give information, my friend, not advice." Mary ruined her effect by slurping the last of her soda. "It's your future, and it isn't fixed."

"Thanks for the information, anyway." Sylvie attempted a glare. "Even if I didn't ask you to do a reading on me."

"That's what friends are for." Mary smiled. "Although, if I'm right…" She indicated the pink candle burning merrily. "You might as well go with red and have some fun."

Pink roses mean friendship, red roses mean passion, mused Sylvie, lighting the bright red jar candle later that afternoon. What a reputation that color had—fiery red, fiery kisses, burning metaphors in crimson-covered romance novels.

Blood.

He probably wasn't coming back.

She glanced over to where Leonard Thibodeaux,

who drew the pictures that hung over each book section, sat hunched in the corner. He remained quiet and still with his drawings, but for an unfortunate facial tick, which medication could only partially control. If he noticed the cinnamon scent in the air, it didn't bother him, so she went back to her accounts. This was what she'd come to—getting worked up over a onetime customer, when once she could have smelled his transience as if it were cheap after-shave. No wonder she didn't date anymore.

A crunching of clamshells outside announced the hearse as it turned into the parking lot. Her glance of anticipation became an openmouthed stare. This time the hearse was definitely not empty—a tangle of arms and legs and bald heads pressed against the long windows. Then the vehicle swung into a space in front of her shop, and she could see only the front windshield. The stranger from this morning sat in the driver's seat, busying himself with the trivialities of brakes and keys. And in the passenger seat sat a smooth-headed mannequin. It wore nothing but a pair of sunglasses, its plastic figure as bare as its head.

Mannequins! Her relief about the load of body parts warred with confusion. A mysterious past, Mary had said. Mysterious she could handle, but *this?*

The ringing of bells on the shop door announced his entrance—and so did a tingling in her stomach, as if the air pressure had just dropped. She tried not to look at him differently, despite Mary's predictions, but he *was* attractive. Surely his easy grin of greeting, the casual self-assurance of his bared chest and his ponytail, couldn't come from an indecent soul!

Then again, judging books by their covers was notoriously dangerous. Remember Eddie.

She only realized that she'd been smiling when the smile faded. Apparently noticing her seriousness, the stranger backpedaled away from the counter. "Whoa!" he said. "I hate it when that happens!"

"I'm sorry." She was amused by the mock consternation in his gray eyes. "It wasn't you, really."

"I don't know. Let's experiment." He deliberately stepped closer to the counter, studying her expression, then carefully backed away from it, then stepped forward again. When her mouth turned up at his antics, he released a sigh of relief. "Must've been a fluke. For once." And he leaned on the counter, sheets of brown parchment in one hand.

"What've you got?" she asked, trying to drag the conversation back onto logical ground. The effect of his presence alone unsettled her—she hardly needed this verbal confusion, as well!

"That's a pretty personal question, isn't it?" He ducked his head. "After all, ma'am, we hardly know each other!"

She snatched the papers from him while he grinned at his own joke. "'Experience the Horror,'" she read out loud from the gothic print. Then she glanced up. "That's advertising?"

"I wouldn't want to get sued for false claims," he called over his shoulder. That was all? He was leaving? No, just leaving the leaflet with her, wandering back to the corner where Lenny sat with his drawing pad on his lap. For a moment she worried that the stranger might tease Lenny, whose medication made him seem a bit slow. He'd been taunted about it before. But if the stranger noticed the funny faces Lenny pulled as he drew, he said nothing about them. She felt a rush of gratitude.

Then she looked back at the flier. "Experience the Horror" stood out in larger letters than the rest. "At the edge of the Stagwater Swamp, shrouded in Spanish moss and mystery, lies the old Deloup House. Deserted? Perhaps not. Dare to experience the chilling secrets that lie within its aged walls...and know Terror!"

Beneath that came hours of operation, which spanned most of October, adult and children's admission prices, and a map with directions from the north end of the Lake Pontchartrain Causeway. "Only 40 minutes from New Orleans," the ad promised. And at the bottom was a picture of a howling black wolf within a circle, as if silhouetted against the full moon.

The next page repeated the logo and promised "The Legend of the Deloup House." A quick scan showed her that it was two pages long; she decided to save it for future reading. After that came a sheet that looked all too familiar to her, because of the words Press Release Press Release Press Release running across the top of the page. She immediately looked at the part of the heading that said Contact.

"Rand Garner," it read, and included a phone number.

She looked up from the parchment and studied the man, who was, in turn, watching Lenny. Rand. He didn't look like a Randy, though she could imagine the cracks he would probably make if she called him that.

"Rand?" she asked, and he flashed her that already-familiar grin.

"In the flesh," he agreed. "Does it all come clear now? I'll let you display any of it, free of charge."

"A haunted house." She tested the words, and with a last glance at Lenny's picture Rand Garner came back to the counter.

"A haunted house *attraction*," he corrected, his voice taking on a theatrical lilt. "And, madame, I am inviting everyone to visit in about two months, for a small fee. But let me warn you—it is not for the weak of heart! The horrors that lurk within the Deloup House's halls…" He shuddered dramatically. "Monsieur Deloup was cursed, you see, and it is said he still stalks his prey in the Stagwater Swamp, either in his mortal, human form, or as the beast he must become each month!"

Actually, every twenty-eight days, Sylvie thought, but that was picky. "Gee, I've lived here a year, and I never heard of this legend."

He didn't miss a beat. "That's because it's a brand-new legend. It is said—now—that lycanthropy has driven Deloup into unspeakable madness. The rotting walls of the house—rotting, yet fire-code-approved, I might add—tremble with the cries of his evil minions and the lost souls of his many victims!" As he finished, Rand dropped his voice, and for a long moment his silvery eyes held her transfixed. She shivered.

There was something frightening about this man, but something equally sexy, as well. *Definite romantic possibilities?* The tang of cinnamon warmed the air around them.

"Monsters?" A third voice broke the spell Rand had cast; Lenny Thibodeaux had approached without their noticing. A sandy-haired, average-size man in his mid-thirties, Lenny stammered slightly when the twitch came. "R-real monsters?"

"Rand Garner, this is Leonard Thibodeaux," she said quickly, hoping this haunted-house stuff wouldn't scare Lenny. "Lenny, this is Rand."

"No, Len, they're fake monsters," Rand admitted easily, and she relaxed. "I build them. I make rubber masks and paint them, the same way you've drawn this...banshee?" He leaned closer to the picture tucked under Lenny's arm and whistled his admiration. Sylvie cocked her head to see it better. She wouldn't have thought a person could draw a spirit that was recognizably a banshee, but...

"That's really good!" she exclaimed, and Lenny ducked his head with pleasure.

"I made it for you," he admitted, pushing the pad onto the counter. "To g-go with the others."

"Only if you let me pay you for it," she insisted, and as always he claimed he'd take payment only in books. In the meantime Rand had slowly turned around, taking in the framed picture of the corpse-through-a-magnifying-glass over the mystery section, the winged unicorn over the fantasy books, and the embracing couple over the romance section.

"You did all these?" he asked, and Lenny nodded shyly. "Listen, do you think I could hire you to do some pictures for my house?"

The delight that lit Lenny's face was suddenly darkened with suspicion. "The haunted house?" he asked.

"It's just the old Jacobs place. I bought it last spring. No monsters—Scout's honor." Rand held up three fingers, his solemnity belied by the hint of a dimple in his tanned cheek. With his long hair and unbuttoned shirt, he couldn't have looked less like a Boy Scout.

But Lenny smiled widely. "Yeah, I would. I've got to go t-tell my mother. Thank you!"

"No, thank *you!*" called Rand with a grin while Lenny backed excitedly out of the shop. Only once the bells on the door had quieted again did he turn back to Sylvie.

"Skeptical?" he asked when she remained silent. "I'm honorable. Brave...um...honest..."

"A Scout with a terribly memory," she supplied, ignoring the niggling worry about his incredible appeal. Nobody had appealed to her in a long time; she didn't completely trust it. Remembering his spiel, she added, "And for future reference, it's *mademoiselle*, not *madame.*"

"I'm very glad to know that." He leaned closer. Again his pale eyes caught and held hers. They reminded her of something....

The clock, chiming five, spoiled the moment.

"I bet," he said softly, "you have to close the shop now or you'll turn into a pumpkin."

"My car turns into a pumpkin," she corrected. And I've got this sudden urge to go to a ball.... On the one hand, she didn't date anymore. On the other hand, fate had taken the time and trouble to throw this intriguing man her way. "But I lose a lot of shoes."

"I'd hate to see you go barefoot on my account," he said, seemingly as a prelude to his departure. "You're here every day, huh?"

"Almost every weekday."

"Good." He began to move away. Then he raised his eyebrows at her, and she realized she wasn't smiling. Hardly unusual, really.

Suddenly he narrowed his eyes purposefully and stepped forward again. She grinned, recognizing his earlier experiment.

"What a responsibility," he mused. "If I have this effect—" And then the phone rang.

Damn, damn, double damn! Don't go, she thought—but he was shrugging, waving...leaving. Damn!

With a sigh, she picked up the phone. "Under-Cover, new and used books." She watched Rand swing into his hearse and reclaim his sunglasses from the mannequin beside him.

"Hi, Syl, Brie. You're coming to dinner tonight, right?" The hearse drove off, its load of plastic people veiled by chalky dust.

"Sure—I want to tell you about something." Or

someone. With the phone between her chin and shoulder, Sylvie keyed the cash register to run its closing tape, then picked up Rand's press release. Don Thomas, over at the print shop, had really done a good job with it. "Anything I should bring?"

"A silver bullet," said Brie.

"What?" She could hardly hear over the chattering register.

"Oops—Steve's here. Gotta go."

"Brigit—" But her sister-in-law had already hung up. Was she having Lone Ranger fantasies, or did everyone have monsters on the brain? "Cries for help from lost—and lonely—souls," promised Rand's press release. "Vengeful spirits, winged demons, evil witches...."

She stared at those last two words, the warmth of his recent company draining from her. She pinched out the red candle. Evil witches. What had Mary said earlier? *As long as stories about wart-nosed, evil hags titillate the masses,* there would be trouble for real witches.

Sylvie raised a hand to her chest and felt the outline of the silver pentagram she wore—point up—beneath her own blouse.

Real witches—like her.

He'd met someone new today. Now he wished he had not allowed himself the pleasure. He'd used to like meeting new people, used to like socializing. He still did, in fact, with an almost desperate intensity. The more alone he felt, the more he enjoyed the com-

pany of others, the pretense that he was still one of them.

But he was alone.

God, was he alone.

He still liked to laugh, to joke, to be with other people. But an invisible wall separated them now. His secret. And it was dangerous. Not just to him, but to them. Ever since...ever since The Change...

His job necessitated some contact with others, but, as much as he enjoyed the company, he wished he didn't have to associate with anyone.

Every person he met was now potential prey.

And the crescent moon grew rounder every night.

CHAPTER TWO

Crescent Moon

Puritans had stereotyped witches as either beautiful nymphs or ugly hags, Sylvie had decided once, because both temptresses and wise women made men nervous. In reality, there was no dress code. Witches, male or female, could be of any appearance.

Despite that, Brigit Conway Peabody was the spitting image of a young, beautiful witch. A riot of fiery curls tumbled around her heart-shaped face, from which smoky blue eyes confronted the world. When she met Sylvie at the door that evening, determination lit those eyes.

"I'm so glad you're here," she breathed. "You are not going to believe this!"

"I'm fine, how are you?" said Sylvie, belatedly pulling the scarf off her head so that her hair feathered free.

"Hi, sis!" called Steve, stepping into the hallway from the kitchen with a soft drink in his hand. Brother and sister looked very much alike—oval faced, brown haired, brown eyed, serious. "You won't believe what I heard today!"

Brie sent Sylvie a significant look and swept past

her husband into the kitchen, calling, "Dinner's almost ready. Make yourself at home!"

"I'll try." Sylvie gave Steve a half hug as she passed him on her way to the homey dining room. She knew their home like the back of her hand. Even if she hadn't spent large amounts of time here—which she had—the layout of her brother and sister-in-law's craftsy home mirrored her own. They had opposite sides of a duplex. "What was it this time, Stevie? The paperboys actually want to be paid? People like the comics better than the editorials?"

"No, the medical examiner finally got word from the FBI lab about the Gareaux body—you know, there was some discussion about whether he really was killed by dogs." He'd been proud of breaking that story, because the weekly *Stagwater Sentinel,* which he edited, found so little news to break. "So anyway, they ran all these fancy tests, and guess what they found?"

As she waited for the answer, she sank into one of the dining room chairs—an antique that Brie had restored. The antique table was already set with Brie's hand-thrown dishes and handmade napkins on top of a hand-loomed tablecloth, all in red tones.

"They don't know!" crowed Steve, plopping into another chair.

"That's not exactly true, hon," Brie called from the kitchen. "Tell her what you told me."

"She'll get one of her crazy ideas," Steve called back. Then he added, "No offense."

"Tell her and find out," Brie challenged.

"All right, here goes. There were some impressions of dog teeth, but there were more impressions of human teeth, okay? Human saliva, human hair, but—get this—wolf fur, too. Apparently whoever—I know, I know, or whatever—did this is what they call a secretor, so if they get a blood sample from a suspect, they can match his DNA like a fingerprint. Right now they're looking for a dark-haired Caucasian. Apparently they couldn't find much to say about the wolfie." Steve shook his head, a little frown line marring the bridge of his nose. "The ME asked me not to print too much of this, of course—as if I would. How could I, without sounding like some yellow rag? 'Werewolf Kills Gareaux!'"

"Gee," said Sylvie, "I didn't even have to say it." She remembered the picture on Rand Garner's advertisement for the haunted house, a black wolf baying at the moon, and suppressed a shiver. Eerie coincidence.

"I knew you were going to, though." Steve pointed a finger at her in an affectionate accusation. "This is the sort of thing you used to write about out on the West Coast. Speaking of which, I've got another assignment for you."

"Steve, could you help me with this roast?" Brie called from the kitchen, so the conversation went no further as he excused himself and went to assist her.

Almost as soon as he went into the kitchen, Brie came out, carrying bowls of squash and green beans. "So, what do you think?"

"I think it deserves investigation," admitted Sylvie. Human hair and wolf fur? Wolf fangs? Sure, she was a witch. She'd been lucky enough to recognize the natural energies that thrummed within the breeze and pulsed from the earth. With Brie's help, she was learning to harness and direct those energies. She liked to think of her deity as being equal parts male and female, and to worship on a lunar-based schedule. But she certainly didn't believe everything that hinted at the occult. There were limits! "I don't remember ever running into this before. I've heard lycanthropy exists, but—"

"There you go again," chided Steve, emerging from the kitchen with a platter of roast beef. "If Brigit has nightmares, I'm blaming you."

"*But*, it exists as a mental disorder," finished Sylvie more loudly, for emphasis. "People with the disorder sometimes believe they're wolves. But they don't turn into anything."

Brie raised an eyebrow at her while Steve carved the meat and put some on Sylvie's plate. "Just because people won't admit something exists, though..."

"You," Steve told her, "are going to be as weird as my sister if you don't watch it." But Brie had made her point.

Sylvie knew that a lot of people thought that ghosts weren't real, that psychic powers were a hoax, that witches didn't exist. Or if they thought witches did exist, they saw them as evil, like the one Rand Garner was advertising.

"I was thinking of having Mary and Cy over this

Friday.'' Sylvie said it lightly, as if to change the subject, but she kicked Brie under the table. ''Do you think you could get away from this idiot for a few hours? We could watch some videos or something.'' They might also discuss the possibility of something supernatural going on.

''I don't think a few hours will kill him,'' agreed Brie, kicking Sylvie back. Steve glanced from his sister to his wife, then shrugged in agreement. It was done, then. One problem momentarily taken care of. But as for the other... Evil witches. Mary would go berserk when she heard that. She would probably rush right over to the Jacobs place—the old Deloup House, now—and force some education down Rand Garner's throat in her one-woman antidefamation crusade.

Sylvie didn't like that idea; the books he'd bought would educate him just fine. But maybe she could follow them up, just to be sure....

''Oh, yeah!'' exclaimed Steve, who'd been frowning for some reason. ''I almost forgot—that job I mentioned. I got a press release today about a haunted house opening in town this fall, and I thought maybe you could do a story or two on it. I mean, with your extra spook degree and all...''

''Mythology and superstition,'' she told him coolly, inwardly reeling at the coincidence. Then again, arcane theory held that there was no such thing as coincidence. Maybe destiny had something in mind for her and Rand Garner.

And maybe there was a connection between the

Gareaux murder and the wolf logo for Rand's haunted house?

She sawed violently at her slice of roast beef. Coincidence. That was all.

The old Jacobs place rivaled neither Tara nor Twelve Oaks, but it was the closest thing to elegance Stagwater had. A long circular drive, chalky white, curved inward through iron gates dulled green by vines. Several huge oak trees, dripping with dusty gray Spanish moss, shadowed the overgrown front yard. Even driving slowly, she could hardly tell the weeds from the original foliage, but she suspected azalea bushes also bordered the drive. No blossoms, though. It was too late in the summer for that.

Which was probably just as well, considering the effect Rand Garner was trying to achieve.

The Jacobs house had been pale blue when she'd moved to Stagwater last year—she remembered seeing bits of broken gingerbread latticework jutting up over the trees and thinking it a shame that the house had fallen to ruin. The only way it could have changed color was through a fresh coat of paint. But the shadowy gray color, chipped and water stained, did not look new. Shutters hung askew, and where windows gaped unshuttered, shards of broken glass glittered evilly. Some of the windows were boarded over, and one looked as if someone had pried the boards off.

She braked her Pinto, closed the windows and got out slowly, remembering to leave her scarf on the parking brake. In the shade of the house and the oaks, humidity and heat clung close to her, giving the afternoon an unnatural stillness, despite the ever-present chirring of insects and birds. When she looked up she noticed that the latticework had changed. Now it resembled spiderwebbing more than gingerbread.

If the Deloup House looked this eerie in broad daylight, it must be very convincing at night!

Faintly, from inside, she could hear the strains of Bach's *Toccata and Fugue in D Minor.*

With Steve's assignment as incentive, she'd called Rand to set up this interview. Despite her wary anticipation, she got only his answering machine, and the voice on the tape sounded like Count Dracula's. His call to confirm the appointment had reached her answering machine, as well. And in the near-week that had passed, he hadn't returned to the bookstore.

She ascended the front steps, which looked as if they would collapse even under a child's weight. Yet they didn't even creak, and neither did the front porch. Rust dulled the door knocker—but since it was in the shape of a wolf's head, metal lips curled back from metal fangs, she suspected it had come with the house's new owner.

Nice touch... Little details like that would really give his "legend" credibility.

The door creaked open under the weight of her first knock, but the shadowy foyer stood empty. The air felt slightly cooler. Organ music trembled through the house. It squashed her questioning "Hello?" to silence beneath it.

She stepped inside and shut the door.

The foyer's wallpaper hung in shreds, as if some great claw had torn at it, and the antique mirror near the door was cracked, reflecting a dozen wary-eyed Sylvies. Chains and padlocks hung on the doors that flanked the room; nylon cord roped off the rounded stairwell, which curved upward, most of its stairs missing. Above her, a cobwebbed chandelier decorated with bloodred crystals hung precariously. She stepped quickly out from under it. And splotches of dark brown stained the once-red carpeting. According to the legend Sylvie had read, this would be where Rodolfe Deloup, in wolf form, had torn out the throat of his fiancée, whose timing had been very, very bad. It was despair at destroying the one thing he held dear, the legend claimed, that had driven Deloup into utter madness.

The strains of Bach had thundered to their crashing conclusion, and she drew in a breath to call out.

The howl of a wolf, coming from everywhere and nowhere, tore her voice away.

Then a woman's voice asked, "Sound good?"

"What?" asked Sylvie, turning. She saw no one.

"Okay, then," said the voice, clearly in answer to something Sylvie hadn't heard. "But I don't know if I can get any more bass out of this system without bringing the walls down." Pause. "Yeah, right."

Odd, that the disembodied voice should have a Yankee accent. "Hello?" Sylvie called loudly. "I'm here for the interview!" She heard a faint answer, like someone yelling a response from far away. Then the disembodied voice said, very clearly, "Rand says he'll be right down, and to hold your horses. What? Oh, for Pete's sake, Garner, where's your sense of humor? Serves you right for not turning off your mike before you bellowed at her."

Silence cloaked the foyer again—until one of the doors creaked slowly open, oversize padlock, rusted chains and all. With the eerie buildup, she half expected Rand to jump out at her as he had from the hearse, maybe wearing some horrible mask. Instead, he leaned into the foyer, his smile of recognition prompting her own.

He'd managed to get her adrenaline pumping, anyway.

"Hi there," he greeted. "You're standing on poor Helena, you know."

She looked down at the brown stain beneath her feet. Helena had been Deloup's murdered fiancée. Supposedly. "It's kind of hard not to."

"Well, you know those Frenchwomen—they get around." The door opened wider, and he joined her in the hallway. Today he wore a clean white work shirt, neatly buttoned, but he wore it over sweaty, dusty jeans, and a light sheen of perspiration clung to his tanned neck and jaw, his arms and hands. His ponytail hung limp in the heat. He also wore a headset, which explained the strange, one-sided conversation she'd heard. "So do you. Mild-mannered bookseller by weekday, intrepid reporter by weekend." He didn't seem to mind.

"I was a journalist before I moved here. Now I

free-lance for my brother sometimes,'' she admitted. "And a friend's watching UnderCover. It's only Friday."

"Like I said. Weekend." Even as she felt herself responding to his mischievous dimple, he turned his attention to the headphone. "I've got that interview, Terry. Why don't you start editing the Helena sequence? We'll finish the sound check later."

"Okay," said the disembodied voice, and the atmosphere changed faintly—the sudden absence of white noise.

Rand flung his arms wide to indicate the simulated decay around them. Sylvie dragged her mind away from sudden, detailed thoughts of being held in those arms. "So, would you like the grand tour, *mademoiselle?*"

"Sylvie." She bit her lip when he stepped beneath the chandelier. Its chain links looked none too solid. "Um…"

He followed her gaze. "Oh, that? No need to worry. Come here." When she hesitated, he widened his gray eyes in an amused dare. It was his house, of course. He'd simulated this decay himself. So she stepped forward; when he touched her arm, to position her in the right spot, warm energy caressed her. "Now, let me get the right remote control," he muttered, poking around in his tool belt. "Okay. Watch the chandelier." And he looked up at it.

So did she.

With a clatter of crystal, the chandelier dropped.

She tried to duck out of the way, but bumped into

Rand, who was still smiling up at the thing. He caught her with one arm against the warm expanse of his shirted chest to keep her from falling. The chandelier stopped its descent perhaps two feet above their heads, and hung there, quivering malevolently.

How long had it been since a man had held her in his arms? He smelled intriguingly of wood chips, turpentine and musk. Maybe this *was* destined, after all.

He looked casually back from the chandelier, his nose almost touching hers. "Welcome to the Deloup House."

The tour fascinated her. Every eerie set somehow revolved around the tragic Deloup story that Rand had created. There was the den, with dusty books about werewolves and monsters spread across the broad desk, and religious texts strewn beside them. "This is where Rodolfe searches desperately for some cure for his affliction," Rand explained, giving the legend a surprising sense of reality even as he had Sylvie rub her hand across fake dust that wouldn't smear away. "He stares at the books, turning pages, muttering— and he lunges at anyone he sees, demanding they explain why this happened to him. You'd be surprised how unsettling it is, to have a deranged person come at you. Or, I should say, you *will* be surprised."

"Rodolfe will be in here?" she asked, considering the claustrophobic effect of the ceiling-high bookshelves and the boarded-up windows. Dusty cobwebs enshrouded everything. Rand had explained that he made them from spun plastic, melted much as sugar was melted for cotton candy.

"In one form or another." He grasped her long-fingered hand in his strong and callused one and led her to a hallway almost hidden by the shelves. "C'mon."

"How are the…um, customers…going to know all this? Not everyone will read the legend."

"I prefer the word 'victims.'" Rand smiled evilly, pausing before another corner. "And they'll have guides. Here—" He let her go first into a stark brick-walled room with manacles driven into one of the walls. "Here is where Rodolfe used to chain himself before the full moon, back when he cared who he hurt. Before Helena. I'm particularly proud of the claw marks. You can see just how far the chain reached, see?" He crouched to indicate the floor.

She sank beside him and touched one of the indentations scratched into the flagstone. It took little imagination to envision a man in the agonies of transformation. He would pull at the chains first, worrying them like an animal in a trap. When that didn't work and the pain took over, he would try to crawl away. Chain pulled taut, he would dig at the stones for purchase, again and again, ragged nails becoming scrabbling claws. He would try to escape the snarling, howling beast he had become, even as the beast fought the chains. And what would it be like, to finally return to his human form, huddled on those cold stones, knowing what he was, knowing what he would always be?

She snatched her hand back from the flagstone—
fake flagstone, damn it!—and took a deep breath. Ye
gods, this was like psychometry! But no, even at her
instincts' height, she'd never been psychic.

Close beside her Rand watched, head cocked, silver
eyes intense. "Are you okay?"

She nodded, her regulated breathing stabilizing her.
She felt as if she'd just emerged from a trance. "I'm
fine, really. It's just all so real. How did you come
up with all this? I mean, the detail!"

The dimples returned; his eyes became merely gray
again, and he stood. He took her hands and lifted her
to her feet as if she weighed nothing. "I was scared
of clowns as a kid, until my mom bought me a
makeup kit. Once I figured out what clowns really
were, I started looking behind the masks of all the
other scary stuff, too. Vampires. Mummies. Politi-
cians."

"So it's all theater to you," she clarified for the
sake of the article. "All make-believe."

He gave her a funny look. "This is the wolf man
we're talking about, not Ted Bundy."

But that didn't explain how he'd gotten so deeply
into the psyche of a "wolf man" that he could create
something as detailed as this.

The thought hung with her as he showed her the
hidden passages—a ladder up a fireplace, a catwalk
over the destroyed chapel—that would allow actors
to confront guests at every turn. It faded, but didn't
vanish, when he showed her the crypt where Deloup
buried the remains of his victims. Their mangled

ghosts would put in an appearance when the house opened, he explained. He brought her to the basement prison where Deloup's servants kept any transients they could catch—people who wouldn't be missed—to feed their master at his whim. "Now that he's crazy, he doesn't need to be a wolf," Rand informed her. She wondered if he noted his own use of the present tense.

And then he showed her the witches' circle.

Black curtains, frosted with cobwebbing, draped the windowless room. Tall candle trees stood in each corner, dripping candles in each—bloodred in the eastern corner, white in the south, gray in the west and midnight black in the north. So he'd decided to use the Celtic tradition, she thought, numb; primary colors were probably too upbeat for his taste. Drawn on the floor in chalk was the most intricate circle she had ever seen, replete with ancient symbols, half of which even she couldn't have translated. In the middle of the circle stood an altar of black marble—although it couldn't be real marble, it still looked cold and forbidding—with a bowl-like indentation in the middle. The proper tools lay on it: an incense burner to represent fire, a chalice to represent water, a black-handled knife, or athame, to direct power, but...

She stepped closer, staring. Rand was continuing his story, saying something about Deloup hiring an evil witch to try to remove the curse, and how that only increased the sacrifices. He didn't realize that he'd finally succeeded in horrifying her. But it wasn't the sort of horror he'd been trying for.

Traditionally, the athame was never used to cut anything, lest it be ruined for magical purposes, but this bloody knife looked as if it had been wielded in a massacre. He'd filled the chalice with fake blood!

"This is all wrong," she said softly, picking up the stained athame. To her disgust, it wasn't fake. He must have found it in an antique store, or a flea market. For all she knew, it had belonged to a witch at one time. *Magical tool becomes theater prop.* With an effort, she kept her voice steady. "It's all wrong. Didn't you read those books I sold you?"

"I skimmed them," he admitted. "All I needed was the illusion of reality. The illustrations gave me that." A little knowledge was indeed a dangerous thing.

"The illustrations never showed this kind of altar, did they? And those symbols around the circle— where in all creation did you come up with these? *Doctor Faustus?* You have no idea what you might be inviting in!" She tried to scuff at one of the symbols with her foot, but it was painted on.

"You're joking, right?" His expression hovered near a smile, waiting for her cue to commit itself.

"No, I'm not. The house, the props— Okay, we all need to recognize the dark side or it will get out of control, and you're providing a safe channel. But this circle!" How could she make him see what he'd done? "It's sick!"

"It's supposed to be sick." His tone had taken on that flat note he'd used when explaining that there were no "wolf men." "It's a haunted house. *Nice* haunted houses don't sell."

"But you've taken something positive and made it—" She spread her arms helplessly; no fitting word came to her. "Witches don't perform sacrifices, Rand. They don't drink blood. This is wrong!"

He's stiffened now. "You don't know that…and really, who's going to care?"

"Witches will!"

"Maybe I should print a disclaimer. 'Scenes in this house are not based on real people and events.'" He rolled his eyes.

"Isn't it true?"

He took her by the shoulders—the stereotypical sane-male-soothing-hysterical-female pose. She fought against the seductive energy that flowed through her at his grip, fought against his scent. "It's just make-believe, Sylvie. There are no witches."

Damn. Slipping a finger inside the collar of her T-shirt, she caught the chain that held her pentagram and pulled it out to dangle between them. "You're wrong."

He stared at the pendant, then at her, his jaw setting in anger. His eyes glinted, and he lowered his hands. Just as well. His energy no longer tingled—it pushed at her. "I think you'd better leave," he said.

"I'm sure we can discuss—"

"There's nothing to discuss." No hint of his earlier playfulness remained. "Get out."

They hadn't finished anything. Whatever had brought this dark man into her life remained unfulfilled. But it went against her ethics to stay there un-invited.

Even if their meeting *was* destined, he had the right to refuse destiny.

"Think about it and call me," she said softly, putting the poor, painted athame back down on the mockery of an altar. Her chest hurt from the need to say more...but he wanted her gone.

So she left, Rand trailing her. When she stepped outside, even the drowning heat and humidity seemed less oppressive. Climbing into her car, she rolled down her window and allowed herself one last look at the man in the open doorway.

Rand stood in the double shade of house and trees, shadows lengthening his jaw, darkening his face, so that only his eyes appeared light. She suddenly wondered what Rodolfe was supposed to look like, and suspected she knew. Maybe it was safer to leave. But he seemed more territorial than threatening....

Oh, why try to read him? If she had any talent left, she could have avoided this fiasco. Throwing her Pinto into gear, she accelerated out of there.

CHAPTER THREE

Gibbous Moon

"The man's hiding something," drawled Cypress Bernard from the yellow cushions of one of Sylvie's two wicker hanging chairs. A dusky-skinned woman with black eyes, heavy black hair and a stubborn jaw, Cy was the most down-to-earth member of the group. "You say you're a witch and he gives you the brush-off? He's afraid you'll use hocus-pocus and find him out, that's all. Good riddance to him."

"He didn't seem afraid," insisted Sylvie, already regretting that she'd brought up the subject. But she'd been so comfortable, with her friends circled about her living room, that she'd confessed about her interview.

"Then what *did* he seem?" prompted Brie, arranging the silver candlestick, carved wooden box and silver goblet that Mary unpacked.

Sylvie, nestled in the butter-colored mama-san chair, rolled her shoulders in a shrug. "I have no idea." The others, friends that they were, didn't comment further. She was supposed to be the empath of the group, and only Brie—her first teacher—had ever seen proof of her ability. Luckily, witches weren't ones to demand "proof."

Brie made friends quickly but, normally a loner, Sylvie was often amazed by how close she and the two Louisiana women had become after barely a year. Much of the credit for that lay with her sister-in-law. It was Brie who, while building UnderCover's shelves, watched Sylvie's customers for fellow witches. It was Brie who invited Cypress and Mary to a Midsummer ritual, and who talked Sylvie into joining the celebration.

Sylvie hadn't wanted to go—she'd lost the lifelong instinct that had connected her to the world in ways physical senses couldn't hope to duplicate, and she'd never been very social. Besides, she couldn't imagine what the four women, Wiccan or not, could possibly have in common. They were as different as the points on a compass! Of them, Brigit was the only born-and-bred witch, Celtic to the core and able to raise and direct energy almost effortlessly. Why should she burden herself with less-experienced practitioners? Cypress's great-grandmother—a swamp witch, Sylvie suspected, though Cy rarely mentioned the woman— had introduced her to the rudiments of earth magic, laced with hints of *Voudun*. Spell casting itself interested Cy very little, though when necessary she could manage energy as competently as she managed accounts. She was establishment—and Mary, the rogue child of a large, Catholic family, was anti-establishment. Mary was naturally psychic, in the same way Sylvie was—had been—naturally empathic, and her interest in holistic healing had first made her aware of Wicca. But Mary had never found a coven she felt comfortable with, and so picked up what she could from books and the occasional class at New Age stores. What could women like that—a married craftswoman, a corporate executive and a massage therapist—possibly find to like in one another...or in a bookseller with a broken heart and no trace of her former abilities?

And yet...

They had clicked, as surely and quickly as Brie and Sylvie had first clicked several years earlier. Rather than complicate matters, their distinct backgrounds and personalities—for abilities were directly connected to personalities—complemented one another like a magical four-part harmony. Sylvie's distance balanced Mary's passionate subjectivity. Cypress's earthiness grounded Brie's fiery energy. Together, they became four pieces of a whole—a circle. How could such interdependence not lead to the closest of friendships?

Still, tonight, Sylvie was glad to escape to the kitchen for some spring water, away from their concern. She sometimes suspected Brie had engineered the first meeting specifically for her—but a person could only take so much support! Besides, since she was still unsure about her own emotions concerning Rand Garner's anger today, she would just as soon avoid their curiosity.

When Sylvie opened the refrigerator door, the light lit up the kitchen. Where Brie's and Steve's place sported bright colors, especially reds, Sylvie's displayed pastels and contained as much glass as she could find. Though not the craftswoman Brie was, she'd installed cabinet doors with glass panels in her kitchen, painted the cabinets themselves yellow and replaced her stainless-steel sink and faucet with a lemony Euro-look set. The changes brightened her white floor and counters without crowding the room. She'd done her whole duplex with similar touches, and she approved of the result here. She liked the sense of spaciousness.

Water, she reminded herself, opening the refrigerator, but the momentary solitude undermined her concentration. She still felt weighed down by today's scene at the haunted house. Wind chimes sang on her back porch, but she hardly heard them, she was so busy reviewing what she'd said, wondering if she should have acted differently. Was Rand hiding something? She'd honestly thought there was something special about him, but she might well have been wrong. Again. Maybe he was just a sexy man with a talent for drawing smiles from her.

The phone on the wall rang, startling her out of her reverie. She shivered in the frigid air, yanking out the bottle of water before answering the phone. "Hello?"

"Um…hi. This is Rand. Garner. Rand Garner. The jerk from the haunted house."

She shivered again, although she'd closed the fridge. That voice. "Hello, Rand," she said cautiously, even as Brie peeked around the corner and raised her eyebrows. Sylvie held out the water bottle. Brie pouted, but accepted it and vanished with a flip of her red curls.

"I've been reading those books I bought from you a little more carefully," he continued. As she stared blankly at the night-darkened window of her back door, Sylvie could picture his face perfectly. Narrow jaw. Gray eyes. No dimple, she thought, not at the moment.

Even his imagined face unbalanced her.

"I'm glad." Warily so.

"It's not as weird as I expected, though I'm still not completely at ease.... Is that usual with people?"

"It depends on their level of exposure. Um...Rand, I have guests...." She hated to say it, but she *had* invited them, and they were probably waiting for her. Or listening in. "Maybe we could talk about this later?"

"Tomorrow night at dinner?"

Her imagined picture of him vanished under a surge of expectation, and she found herself staring at her own excited reflection. "A date?"

"I could probably feed you more than one date, but if your heart's set on it..." She could hear that the dimples had returned.

A real date. It had been so long.... "You're sure? I mean, this is some turnabout from this morning."

"Well, it *is* against my better judgment."

She blinked at the phone for a moment; then he laughed. Oh. A joke.

"Actually, I was hoping to ask you out after the interview, but I got sort of...sidetracked. Now I want to make it up to you. So will you accept? Please? You can educate me."

"And you'll change the display?"

"You can educate me," he repeated.

Better than nothing. A real date. "Could you pick me up at the bookstore?"

"Pumpkin time?"

"Exactly."

Brie peeked around the corner again. "Hey, Syl, you're missing a great reading!"

"I'll see you then," she told Rand, ignoring her sister-in-law's raised eyebrows.

"Especially if I see you first. 'Bye, then. Or, as my mother used to say, um… Damn, I knew I should have listened to her."

"Goodbye." Sylvie laughed—actually laughed! Destiny had reasserted itself. She was going to see Rand again.

"See him when?" demanded Brie, grinning as Sylvie hung up the phone.

"Tomorrow night." Sylvie sidestepped her, going back to the candlelit living room. "He's taking me to dinner."

"As long as *you* aren't dinner," cautioned Brie darkly. When Sylvie turned on her, she spread her hands. "Hey, it was Cypress who said he might be hiding something."

"Excuse me," muttered Mary from where she knelt beside the glass-and-wood coffee table. "Could we tone it down?" A spread of tarot cards lay in the pool of candlelight before her. Sylvie perched on the edge of the mama-san for a better look.

"Our focus is the King of Cups, reversed," Mary

explained, sliding a card aside to show the upside-down man. "He hides his true nature. I figure he's the murderer."

"So it's a regular man? I mean, regular for a murderer."

"He's hidden from us by The Moon—illusion, perhaps deceit. And look at that." Mary tapped the lower corner of the card. Beneath a full moon crouched two howling beasts: a dog and a wolf. "They're almost mirroring each other, wild versus tame," she continued softly. "As if it could go either way." Then she pointed at the cross card—what would hinder the murderer. It showed a brown-haired woman on a throne, a raised sword in her hand. The Queen of Swords.

"Me?" asked Sylvie, her stomach tightening.

"I think so, yes," said Mary. "But you're not alone—I'm in a future position. But it's getting late." She began to scoop the spread together, to put the cards away. "We came here to do a real scrying, didn't we?"

"What's wrong?" asked Sylvie, suddenly chilled in the room's near darkness.

Mary put the cards back into their silk bag, then into their wooden box, before meeting her gaze. "Don't tell me you felt something?" she asked challengingly. Stalemate. "The scrying will tell us more than a reading anyway."

They settled around the table and began to breathe deeply to prepare themselves. Mary drew the goblet of spring water in front of her, then waited. Though a trained psychic could see images—scry—in any-thing, she did best with water—and the concentration of the others. Each person, with her own distinct strength, would enhance Mary's abilities.

The candle flame flickered in a sudden draft.

The murder, thought Sylvie, as clearly as she could. It was easy to grow dizzy or distracted at this point, as their joint power expanded. Human teeth marks, canine teeth marks, human hair, wolf fur, murdered on the last full moon....

With a cry, Mary knocked the goblet away and dived back from the spilled water. Candlelight re-flected crookedly through the wet glass.

"What is it?" demanded Brie, taking her arm. "What's wrong?"

"Blood," whispered Mary, while Sylvie sprang up and turned on a lamp. Incandescent light filled the room.

"Calm down, honey," ordered Cypress. "It's just water. You're at Sylvie's, remember? Ground your-self, lady!"

Mary laid her palms on Sylvie's wood floor and took a deep breath, released it, then drew another. When she finally lifted her hands, the strange distance had left her eyes. She glanced from one friend to an-other. "I...um...sensed several things, confused, like in a dream. Someone is very confused, violent...." She shuddered. "It's like a hunger. A blood thirst. He hates it, but it controls him. I almost saw a man's face, but the water went murky, and I realized it was blood...." She wrapped her arms around herself as Brie offered her an afghan from a wicker trunk.

Belatedly Sylvie moved to fetch a towel. The spell was most definitely broken.

"Wait," said Mary, extending her hand to touch the spilled water. She looked up at Sylvie. "Before it went completely dark, I saw the wolf. It felt—like the murderer." She drew a shaky breath. "I think we're dealing with the real thing, friends. I think this is a werewolf."

Rand took Sylvie to a seafood restaurant built on a pier over Lake Pontchartrain. "Listen," he said to the host, "any chance we can get a table with a view? Shrimp boats, sunset lake, ladies' room?"

"I'll...um...see what I can do. If you'd care to wait at the bar?" The host departed with a bewildered glance as Rand innocently gestured Sylvie to a bar stool.

"You enjoy keeping people off balance, don't you?" she asked, hiking herself up onto the seat and smoothing the filmy skirt of her white dress.

He shrugged. "I feel less alone that way."

The female bartender lingered taking their drink orders, and who could blame her? Rand looked particularly good tonight. He wore a loose gray blazer over a blue shirt, with baggy white jeans that almost hid his lack of socks. His sleek ponytail made him look scampish, and his grin even more so. And he radiated an energy that had been mixing with her own, hot and heavy, since he'd arrived at UnderCover to pick her up.

To make the evening particularly nonthreatening, he'd picked her up in a Volkswagen bug—dated, but hardly as odd as his hearse. "I only drive that to haul supplies and to advertise," he explained, when she expressed relief. "Do you know what lousy gas mileage hearses get? It's no wonder that so few corpses take road trips."

Now he said, "So, you're a witch? You know, I've never used that line as a conversation starter before. Oh, sure, change some of the consonants around and it sounds familiar...."

"Shh..." She darted a glance toward the bartender, who looked quickly away, then turned back to Rand. The dimples were back. He probably found her discomfort humorous.

"How do people normally react?" he prompted.

"I haven't really told anybody else...not any nonpagans, at least."

"Why not?"

"Some people don't take it too well."

While he considered that, their drinks arrived. She took a sip of her chilled piña colada, savoring the sweet taste of pineapple and coconut until the bartender stopped drooling and left.

Then Rand asked, "How do you know that if—"

"I've got a friend who is very open about her beliefs. I've seen the problems she had. She's a massage therapist, and when she tried to set up—"

"She's a masseuse!" His pale eyes twinkled.

"Massage therapist."

"There's a difference?"

She took a deep, calming breath. "That's the problem. You hear massage therapist and you think of prostitution. You hear witch and you think of bogeyman, devil worship."

His fingers on her lips silenced her, as did the resulting shiver down her spine. What would they taste like, those fingers?

"So show me how wrong I am," he said softly, brushing her lower lip as he withdrew his hand.

"You'll listen?"

"I'm all ears." He turned his head to show her a nice lobe. "The better to hear you with, my dear."

She hoped.

The host arrived and showed them to a private table next to a window overlooking the water, if not the sunset. At first their conversation centered on food. She decided on boiled shrimp, but he claimed to have a problem with any food that looked back and ordered baked fish. Only when their salads arrived did he assess her steadily and ask, "So, how does a modern American girl grow up to be a witch?"

"It fit," she said easily, truthfully. "All my life I felt different. Separate. I loved nature, and I couldn't stand crowds...." But maybe she'd better avoid the part about her empathy. It had scared some people, how easily she'd read them. It might upset him, as well—and she couldn't even do it anymore! "I was always drawn to stories about magic, the legends of ancient Ireland and the scraps of Celtic customs that still show up on holidays.''

"Like Halloween,'' he guessed, obviously picking a favorite. She wasn't the only one ignoring her salad; his remained untouched, as well.

She nodded. "And the holly and ivy at Christmas. The eggs at Easter. Even Groundhog Day dates back to a Wiccan celebration of early spring.''

He grinned. "I always thought there was something weird about ol' Punxsutawney Phil.''

"I love Groundhog Day. My brother thought *I* was weird. Funny thing is, it's through him that I met Brie. She spent half an evening with me, pulled me aside and asked how I'd ever lasted so long without...'' She paused. *How'd you last this long without shields, kid?* Brie had asked. *You're not an empath, you're a sponge!*

"Without Wicca?'' prompted Rand. "Sounds a bit like a hard sell. Weren't you worried you might get involved with some kind of cult thing?''

"I kept my eyes open,'' she assured him. "And the first—really, the only—rule I learned was 'harm none.' That reassured me, too.''

His gray eyes held hers, suddenly intense. "What about your enemies?''

A third voice said, "Now, who had the fish?'' For a moment she thought Rand meant to ignore the waiter, but finally he looked away. She sat back as if an invisible tie had been cut.

Maybe she shouldn't have told him anything, she mused, barely noticing the plate of fat pink shrimp that was placed before her. He seemed almost angry. Maybe Brie's tradition was right in demanding secrecy among nonbelievers.

"None," she repeated, as soon as the waiter turned to leave. Then she turned her attention to the shrimp, peeling one right after another. Twist off the head, rip off the legs, slide off the shell....

"There does, however, seem to be a loophole for boiled shrimp," Rand noted. When she glanced up at him, startled, he flashed her a lopsided grin of truce.

He would make a smiler of her yet.

"You know, you haven't gotten to the good stuff," he noted, pointing his fork at her. "What about magic?"

"Still interested in love spells?" It was hard not to notice how his profile was taking on a golden cast. They might have missed the sunset, but the light of the rising moon caressed his cheekbones, his jaw, his throat....

"You're sure they're unethical?" he mourned.

"Not even fairy-tale witches used them. Cinderella got new clothes and wheels, but the prince fell in love of his own free will." She imagined her palm tracing the path of the moonlight along his cheek...then turned firmly back to her shrimp. If and when she succumbed to such an attraction, it would be with full awareness of the dangers. She'd traveled this path before!

"Now, the fairy tales I liked," he said after a moment, "were the ones about monsters, giants, trolls...." He began telling her about his early fascination with horror. His expressive eyes and mouth, the tilt of his head, the significant pauses that signaled a punch line—Rand had more charisma than any man she'd ever known. By the time they'd finished dinner and paid the bill, they'd discussed fairy tales and favorite horror novels and were well into a debate about the genre's violent reputation.

"The stuff doesn't just glorify evil and make perfectly natural things like nighttime and cemeteries seem dangerous," Sylvie insisted as they walked out of the restaurant and onto the open pier. The heat had barely relented with the sun's disappearance, and the air felt thick and heavy around them. But the rich, fertile smell of the shadowy woods across the road perfumed even the fishing-trawler mustiness of the air.

"And remote waterside villages," Rand pointed out, and gestured toward the lakeshore, an invitation on his expressive face. "Don't forget the horrible reputation they've gotten."

"And those," she agreed, taking the hand he offered. She liked the shiver of electrical disturbance she felt at his touch. "But the fact that horror stories encourage fear at all…fear is such a negative emotion. Why empower it?"

"Ah, but is that the result?" He sent her a sideways glance, the dimple softening his cheek as they strolled toward the moon. "The majority of horror stories show a character who faces fear and conquers it."

If he'd been pulsating with hot, white light, she couldn't have been more aware of his presence beside her, even as she watched her own sandaled feet traverse the pebbly shoreline. "Not most," she said.

"Sure they do."

"No, most of the characters get skewered, axed, crushed, eaten, electrocuted, mutilated, burned or decapitated. Always with a great geyser of blood…"

He stopped walking, and when she glanced questioningly at him, she found him watching her, head cocked, the barest smile softening his lips…or was that just the moonlight? Around them, insects creaked and toads sang.

"Do you realize," he said, "that we've talked about horror through most of dinner and you haven't said, 'Ew, gross,' even once? You really are different, aren't you?"

Different. Shut out. Distant. Apart from everyone and everything, and maybe unable ever to be connected again.

But maybe not.

"Yes."

"I am, too." He stepped closer to her, pebbles grating beneath his feet. His muskiness mingled with the natural scents of the lapping lake and the woods.

"Good," she breathed, losing her thoughts in his silvery, moonlit eyes.

"Maybe."

The moment hung suspended in the thick, humid air. He ducked his face toward hers, paused as if in consideration, then touched her lips with his. It was barely a whisper of a kiss. He hovered close, and then his hungry mouth covered hers. Energy surged through her entire being, unbalancing her, but not unpleasantly. Her lips parted under his, and she drank him in. His arms encircled her. He held her captive in his embrace, while her own hands skimmed his lean back. Their shared energy built, then lulled, lurking as they parted.

Moonlight danced off his eyes, so near her own.

She smiled.

This time, when their mouths met, they were open, tongues exploring, teeth grazing, one kiss blending into the next. No longer could she sense her energy or his. Instead, an electric mingling of both cocooned them. He held her so tightly to him that it almost hurt. She clutched him just as desperately. His chest crushed her breasts, and as their thighs pressed together she could feel the heat of his arousal. This was getting out of control, but she didn't care. His muskiness enveloped her; his strength empowered her. When his mouth left hers to nuzzle a steamy trail down her throat, she clung to the muscled back of his neck. Her fingers buried themselves in his thick hair. Her own mouth opened soundlessly. He claimed it again. This felt right. Never had it felt so right, not even with Eddie.

Eddie. Like an ill wind, the momentary remembrance of her ex-fiancé cooled her face.

It was enough.

Cast in the eerie light of the moon, Rand's face loomed above hers, silver eyes half-lost in a tangle of loose, shaggy hair. His chest rose and fell as he panted, openmouthed. He was male, savage, un-tamed—and he frightened her.

She drew back from him, struggling a moment until he released her, then backpedaling a few steps until she felt safe enough to stay her flight. Her fluttering heartbeat urged her to run, but she refused, torn. She took a deep breath and tried to gather her own energy about her again, like a cold aura.

He stood still, catching his breath. He rubbed a hand over his face, shook his head. Then he pulled his thick, dark hair back off his face and tied it back into a ponytail.

He looked more like Rand then, and she began to feel foolish. But not foolish enough to stop being wary.

"Come on," he said simply, and they began to walk back along the shoreline to the restaurant and car. His hand brushed the small of her back in order to to guide her over a mushy patch of ground. When it drifted away, she felt bereft and, in confusion, held her hand out to him.

His strong fingers closed around hers, and she relaxed in his warmth. He no longer looked wild. If anything, he looked confused. Resigned. "Sylvie, I'd never hurt you. I want you to know that. Not…not if I could help it."

"I'm sorry."

"Don't be."

"I suddenly…panicked." That was an understatement.

"It happens. We—I—moved awfully fast."

When she reviewed their actions, she felt a blush color her face. She was Sylvie the aloof, Sylvie the controlled. Or she should have been. "Like being possessed." The words came out before she could stop them.

"Or bewitched?" he suggested as they arrived at the Volkswagen.

"It doesn't—"

"Work that way," he finished for her, dimple reluctantly reappearing. "You told me." And he brushed her lips with his own. The softness of his kiss echoed gently down her spine. Had she been temporarily insane, pulling away? If he took her in his arms again, she wouldn't protest...but instead he opened her door for her.

Damn.

"I had a good time," she said when he was belted in and starting the car. "I enjoyed it—all of it."

He flashed her a playfully wolfish grin. "Me, too—particularly the 'all of it' part. I'd like to see you again, but..." He shrugged apologetically, easing the car onto the road. "My schedule's fairly unpredictable this week.... Maybe this weekend?"

Something niggled at the back of her mind. She ignored it. "Friday? Or Saturday?" Or both, if all went well?

He stared at the blacktop revealed by the headlights. "Friday's no good. Saturday?"

"Saturday," she agreed, and settled back to relax in the almost-cool rush of air from her open window. Heavy curtains of tall pine trees bordered the road on both sides, reducing the sky to a narrow strip above them. And the moon…

"In fact, I'll be busy Friday, too," she added, belatedly recalling her circle's planned esbat celebration. She was still missing something, though. "So that works out fine."

"Really?" he said, glancing from the road long enough to study her expression, eyes intent. He looked quickly away.

Finally she placed the niggling at the back of her mind.

He was busy on Friday. Friday was esbat.

And esbat was the full moon.

Full moon tonight.

He quit work early, his dread of the coming night making the moonrise seem sooner than it would be. He didn't want to change again, not when everything was going well. He didn't want…

The Change wouldn't care what he wanted.

He fixed dinner, but he had no appetite. He couldn't stomach any bland, ordinary repast with such a blood feast awaiting him.

No! He wouldn't! He would find a way to stop; he would chain himself up. He started searching for a padlock, burrowing through drawers. His hands, rummaging through kitchen implements, slowed, then stopped. His soul was weak. Even if he found a lock, he wouldn't use it.

Which meant he hated himself not just as a wolf—but as a man, too.

CHAPTER FOUR

Barley Moon

The dusky September sky clung to the sun's last light as Sylvie, with Brie in the passenger seat, pulled out of their side road and onto the blacktop.

Almost nightfall.

Almost moonrise.

"Steve seems worried," Brie mused, casting a glance in the rearview mirror. "Not just because we're going out at night, either. Because it's a full moon."

"After two years with you, he shouldn't be surprised," Sylvie murmured, only half listening. As she accelerated, the moist air blowing in her open window eased from hot to tepid. Woods walled them in on either side—tall pines that were nothing but skinny trunks for the lower twenty or thirty feet, and sprouted branches only toward the top, where they blocked off most of the sky. Nearer the ground, in shadow, blurry underbrush whizzed past just across the drainage ditches.

"I've been subtle. He hasn't noticed a thing," the redhead protested firmly. "The point is, Steve doesn't believe in witches, much less werewolves. And he's worried. If the whole town starts thinking that way…"

She didn't have to finish the sentence. The more people who believed in the werewolf—if there even was a werewolf, Sylvie reminded herself—the stronger its powers would become.

And the less chance that tonight's binding spell would work.

The trees thinned closer to town, making room for UnderCover, the post office and the tiny library. After three lights, all green—that often happened with Brie in the car—the Pinto bounced over the railroad tracks and passed the grocery and video stores and the garage. Only once the woods thickened again did they near the Deloup House.

Sylvie glanced at the shards of latticework visible over the trees as she drove by, haunted by the same thought that had bothered her all week. What *was* Rand doing tonight?

"So, have you heard any more from loverboy?" asked Brie.

"Our date isn't until tomorrow," Sylvie reminded her, not wanting to mention that Rand had come by the store yesterday. In fact, he'd seemed to appear out of nowhere. One minute she'd been discussing her new bookmarks with Don Thomas, the town printer, and the next a wolf whistle had cut through the shop.

And there, in jeans and an oversize shirt, had stood Rand, framed in the doorway against a rainy backdrop. "Opened it slowly," he'd said, his grin wary as he indicated the bells that should have announced his arrival. She'd wondered how long he'd been standing there. "Hello, Mr. Thomas." And he'd held the door while the small, balding printer left with only a nod.

"Don't mind him. He lost his wife a few months back," she'd said, to excuse Don. "He—"

But by then Rand had leaned down and was kissing her. Their mingling energies had curled happily around them, as if her panic by the lake had never happened.

"I know," Rand had said.

Now the tires of the Pinto grated on the gravel at the side of the road; suddenly alert, Sylvie added, "And no, he didn't tell me what he's doing tonight."

But she'd noticed a lock securing the Deloup House's iron gates.

South of Stagwater they turned off the highway and took a rutted back road. The tall, skinny pines surrounding them gradually gave way to huge, ancient oaks draped in Spanish moss. Occasionally Sylvie's headlights, which she'd turned on to combat the deepening dusk, reflected water somewhere off the road. Reaching what appeared to be a dead end on the edge of the swamp, she parked beside Mary's old pickup truck and killed the engine.

For a moment the headlights illuminated an impenetrable tangle of woods beyond a granddaddy oak whose branches bowed low to the ground. When she cut the lights, the world vanished into thick, humid shadows alive with the chirring of toads and insects and the rustling of what were probably small animals.

If Rand wanted a crash course in spooky, he should try the Louisiana swamp at night. Sylvie stepped out of the car into soft, dark dirt. She had to get Rand out of her mind; they had work to do. But what kind of plans could he have had, tonight of all nights?

A hand on her shoulder made her gasp, and she spun around defensively.

Mary, who'd emerged from the shadows, stared back at her in equal surprise, then patted her shoulder reassuringly.

''You expecting someone else?''

He didn't have to look to sense the moonrise. His skin tingled with apprehension, his breath shortened, his heartbeat sped. Of course, it *would.* Wolves' hearts beat more rapidly than humans', didn't they?

He would shut himself up in his den. Fitting, huh? A den? The desperate humor of the thought made him want to cry, but no tears came to his eyes. Wolves didn't cry.

From somewhere outside, the moon pulled at him. He couldn't breathe! Hot, so very hot, he tore at his clothes, peeled off his pants, yanked off his watch, everything…until no more clothes constricted him and he lay, whimpering and panting, atop them. He held his hands in front of him—a man's hands, meant to do work and caress a woman, not to do harm. Yet they cramped into claws, no longer his hands at all. And his head! A seizure inside his skull drove out reason—not in one blessed sweep, no, but in waves. Each wave lasted longer, breaking only long enough for him to realize what was happening, to wish himself dead....

But then, after an eternity and yet far too soon, there were no more breaks, no more reason.

Its lips curled back from canine teeth in a snarl.

Outside, the moon ascended.

Sylvie knelt on the ground beside the fallen log that served as their altar, carefully arranging the last of the black-and-white photographs she'd brought. A circle of hairy-barked cypress trees circled the four women, and she could sense the river. The nearness of the water charged the air and softened the earth. But, luckily, Mary had found a clearing high enough to be temporarily dry.

Ethics and good sense forbade the witches from directing any real harm toward the killer, especially with so little knowledge. What goes around comes around, good intentions or not, and if the killer were a werewolf, he was an already-cursed human. So they'd arrived at a different course of action—a spell to protect the town. Sylvie had spent over an hour going through Steve's picture files at the paper in order to collect photographs showing as many Stagwater residents as possible.

"I sure hope this works," muttered Mary from the shadows outside Brie's flashlight beam as she shoved a fourth and final waist-high stake into the ground and stepped back. Cypress placed a blue pillar candle on it to complete the quarters. "We can't possibly have pictures of everybody."

"The law of contagion," Sylvie reminded her. "A piece of something is as good as the something. This is a majority of Stagwater, so..."

The flashlight beam jiggled while Brie fished in her pocket, then tossed two color snapshots onto the pile. One was a wedding picture of Brie and Steve gazing at each other with a love Sylvie might have resented had she not loved them so much herself. The other was a photo of Mary, Sylvie and Cypress, taken the last time Brie had dragged them to a flea market. Cypress held a big bag of purchases, Mary was trying to peek into it, and Sylvie...as usual, she looked distant, aloof. Alone.

"Just in case," Brie said.

Suddenly Sylvie wished she had a picture of Rand to add to the collection. Of course, that would be pointless if...

She raised her eyes to the eastern sky, where the faint glow of the moon, which had yet to break the trees, blurred the starlight, and shivered.

It kept to the woods. With an animal's instincts, it knew better than to get too close to the light and sounds of civilization. So it circled instead, watching, prowling, sniffing for blood.

The hunger hurt.

When the moon finally rose high enough to top the moss-draped trees and cast the prepared grove in silver light, the witches began their ritual. Blending into the night, Cypress raised her arms as if to embrace the northern sky, welcoming the element of earth before lighting the green candle in front of her. The flicker of light reflected off the gold lamé of her blouse and her ankh earrings.

Sylvie turned to the east, raised her arms and visualized for a moment what the element air symbolized—creativity and intellect. When she lit the yellow pillar candle, more light flooded the clearing, and the darkness began to retreat.

Brie repeated the gesture toward the south, with a red candle for the element fire, and even the shadows began to slink back. Mary's final blue candle, for water, closed the circle, adding its light to their oasis of security within the bayou.

Now, properly prepared, they began to raise their protective energy.

Hunger. It smelled water, but water wouldn't feed it. Then it smelled something else and crept forward. It recognized the river, recognized prey by the river. It watched from the brush, panting, hungry.

Tyrell liked fishing at night, especially during the full moon. Seemed like the fish almost jumped on shore—all he had to do was sit on the tailgate of his pickup and swing 'em in. He had three catfish crowded in his bucket already—good eatin', if his woman cooked 'em up right. 'Course, tonight she might not want to, considerin' how he'd knocked her around a bit.

This stretch of river was slow. Overhanging trees blocked out even the moonlight, and Tyrell could barely see by the light of the lantern hanging off his tailgate. Off in the dark an owl hooted, an animal screeched, toads chirped, crickets sang.

Then they all stopped.

Tyrell took his eyes off his fishing line to look around him. Nothing much to see but a whole lot of dark. Cramped in the metal pail, the catfish cut each other with their fins. Out on the river…

It looked kind of like a log, he thought, floatin' out there. An alligator?

Maybe he should take his fish and leave.

Tyrell hauled in his line, stood up and shut the tailgate of his pickup. He lifted his bucket of fish— he would have liked to bring home more, really give his woman something to complain about, but he wasn't gonna stay, not feelin' as creepy as he did. He walked around the side of the pickup.

A blur of gray fur loomed in front of him, then launched itself directly at him. He didn't even have time to scream.

Silent struggle faltered, then stopped. Snarling gave way to eating.

The bucket rolled down the bank, spilling catfish which flopped back into the river and swam away.

The witches danced the ancient spiral dance, throwing their spinning vortex of power higher and higher until it threatened to escape them. Then they sensed the culmination of their power. As one, they stopped, reached upward, released their creation out of their circle and into the world of others.

Sensation shuddered through Sylvie—a draining, then a shiver despite the heat of the humid night. Done. She sank to the ground, lest she fall. In the bright safety of the candlelight she watched the others do the same, reclaiming strength from the earth beneath them.

As they willed it, so must it be.

Unless they were too late.

She felt so weak from energy loss that when she heard the twig crack behind her, then felt the eyes, she almost didn't bother looking. The expression that whitened Brie's face, across the circle from her, changed her mind.

Slowly Sylvie turned.

A wolf stood not ten feet from their circle, just beyond a cypress tree, its damp muzzle high, sniffing, aimed at *her!* Its thick, slate gray coat seemed to absorb the candlelight; its almond eyes, however, were mirrors.

She should have been frightened. Its eyes never left her.... But weren't a wolf's eyes supposed to be yellow? Oddly enough, this wolf's eyes were silver.

Like Rand's.

Gracefully she rose, her skirt swirling into place about her calves.

The wolf watched her, seemingly intrigued.

"What do you think you are doing?" demanded Brie through clenched teeth.

There were times that weren't mean for thinking.

She took a step nearer the wolf, then another. Its presence drew her.

It began to pant, tongue lolling out, looking for all the world as if it was grinning.

When she extended her hand, the wolf licked its chops and shut its mouth, looking serious again. It sniffed, then cocked its head.

"Fool, get away from that thing," whispered Cy. "You hear me?"

Don't be him, don't be him, don't be him. Brie had made jokes, of course. Some of the evidence had swung that way.

But the unreality of the situation had let it go no further—until now. Something felt too familiar about this wolf, perhaps a smell, perhaps something beyond the boundaries of documentable sensory evidence. And if there could be a wolf here, in the bayou, in the first place, then was it such a leap of the imagination—?

"Rand?" She whispered the name. She didn't want the others to realize her suspicions. But the wolf heard. It—he?—perked its ears forward, as alert as if she'd called it by name.

"Rand." This time she barely mouthed the name, but the wolf still responded, ducked its head, made a whuffing sound. The dampness on its muzzle and ruff looked like water, not blood. Though a huge animal, lean and sleek, it was hardly more threatening than Rand Garner himself.

Until it growled.

"Sylvie, you get back here or I'm going to make

you come back, manipulation or not,'' Brie called softly from somewhere behind her.

Ears back, mirrored eyes slitted, the dark animal growled again, low in its throat. Thoughts of the fictitious Rodolfe and Helena suddenly crowded into Sylvie's mind. How could she have approached this animal? How could she have been so stupid? If it wanted her...

To her confused relief, the wolf suddenly whirled away and vanished into the shadows of the swamp.

It couldn't be him. Not Rand. Not the first man she'd been attracted to since the disaster with Eddie.

''I say we get out of here now,'' said Brie, and Cy seconded it, calling a quick thanks to the elements as she snuffed the candles at each quarter. The light became dusky, then shadowy, then dark. Brie's flashlight cut a swath of feeble brightness in what had reverted to a clearing in the night woods, nothing more.

The temperature seemed to drop.

''You don't think we're safe?'' Mary asked, quickly collecting the candles and photographs before they started back toward the cars. ''It did leave us unharmed.''

Which would argue for the success of their spell, except...

''That wasn't the werewolf,'' Sylvie insisted, only to have her words punctuated by a mournful howl from the swamp. Long, lonely, tremulous...the sound shuddered down her backbone. It was as if she shared the animal's grief. "It was a *wolf* wolf," she added, but with less conviction.

She went through the motions of hugging Mary and Cy goodbye, hardly noticing when Mary disappeared down the dirt track toward her houseboat. Sylvie and Brie climbed into the Pinto, drove behind Cy down the dirt road and out of the swamp.

There had to be a way to prove objectively that the wolf they'd seen was not…the killer. Was not Rand.

The solution, so simple as to be laughable, made Sylvie's distraction evaporate like the cool breeze coming through her open window. She would phone Rand. Sure, it was almost midnight, but she could risk a little rudeness against the crazy suspicions she'd begun to form. She would call him, and if he answered, she wouldn't need to worry any longer.

"Oh, hell," Brie said suddenly. "Mary still has my wedding picture."

"You're sure?" Sylvie slowed but didn't stop. Mary didn't have a telephone, and she wanted to call Rand as soon as possible.

"Yes, I'm sure." Brie muttered a few expletives. "Steve might notice it's gone and get suspicious. You don't mind going back, do you?"

Rather than lie, Sylvie merely slowed enough to pull a tight circle. The Pinto's wheels touched the freedom of the highway oh-so-briefly before its taillights turned toward the blacktop. Home was barely fifteen minutes away. A short detour like this would hardly count to anyone but her own anxiety-riddled self. What difference was there between waking Rand at 12:10 or at 12:30? As long as he answered.

And if he didn't?

It crept along the bank of the river, alert for bear and feral pigs—other predators like itself. The metallic taste of blood filled its mouth, its nose, and yet its kill had not sated it. It needed more. It needed prey. It needed— Head high, it sniffed the air, then listened.

Light footsteps approached the water, expertly skirting vines and exposed roots.

The hunger rose in its throat, roared in its ears. If some human part of its mind protested, it did not comprehend that protest. It knew only what its animal instincts told it.

It crouched to stalk. The prey paused, hesitated— and fled.

The chase was on.

It happened so fast. The headlights caught movement near Mary's truck, but even as Sylvie recognized the blond psychic and leaned on the horn, the attacker was fleeing.

Nothing but a blur of gray, and a last glimpse of a wolf's tail.

Sylvie fought her seat belt, practically falling out her door, letting the Pinto buck and die rather than taking the time to throw it into neutral. The thing, the creature, was gone even before she could round the front of the car. With no more thought for it, she swooped down onto her knees beside the pale figure that lay unmoving in the wash of the car's headlights.

"Mary! Come on, sweetie, be okay!" But Mary wasn't okay. Blood, black in the artificial light, welled from her arm and spattered on her T-shirt. Her hair had pulled free in the struggle, pooling like a blond pillow around her face.

Vaguely aware that Brie was standing over her, aiming her flashlight at the woods and brandishing a tire iron, Sylvie yanked the scarf off her hair and wrapped it as tightly as she could around Mary's injured arm. Then she lifted her friend's bare legs and extended her own leg to pillow them. Raise the feet for shock, right? "There's a blanket in the car," she said to Brie. "We'll wrap her in it and take her to the emergency room."

"No." Mary's words were slurred at first, as if she were waking from sleep. "I hate doctors." She opened her eyes then and stared blearily up at Sylvie. "What—?"

"You almost became wolf chow, kiddo," supplied Brie. "Your arm's gonna need stitches for sure."

Sitting up with a whimper of pain, Mary looked down at the blood-spattered scarf wrapping her arm, then nodded her reluctant permission. Between them, Sylvie and Brie managed to help her over to the Pinto.

"At least it worked," Mary managed to point out as they eased her into the back seat. She winced. "The spell. He didn't kill me."

Tucking the blanket around her, Sylvie stood and reviewed the scene again in her mind. Despite her old reporter's instincts, it remained a blur. But thinking of the werewolf as an attacker recalled something else.

"We have to contact the police," she said, adding reluctantly, "And one of us should stay to talk to them."

Brie exploded, shooting the flashlight beam in an arc around them. "You really are crazy!"

"The sooner they get out here, the better chance they have of catching this…this…"

"Werewolf! You're asking them to come investigate a werewolf!"

For once Sylvie took advantage of her full height. "They'll investigate anyway. We need to give them a chance to do a decent job of it!" She glared down at her sister-in-law; Brie glared right back up. So Sylvie said, "I'll stay."

"No."

"I'll wait in the pickup," Sylvie insisted. "It's practically a tank!"

"Key's under the mat," murmured Mary from the car.

Brie hesitated, then groaned in defeat and leaned into the car to snatch her purse from the front seat. She extracted a pistol; it was so small it looked like a toy. "You know how to use one of these?"

Would it do any good without silver bullets? Sylvie took the weapon and hefted its weight. If nothing else, it would make her feel better. "As soon as Mary's admitted, call the cops and send them here," she instructed, opening the door of the pickup and making sure nothing was lurking inside. "Don't forget!"

For a moment she thought she would have a battle with Brie about who would get into her vehicle last, and thus take the most risk, but Brie's worry over Mary won out. The redhead climbed into the Pinto, ground its gears and swung away.

Sylvie slammed the pickup door, slapped down both locks and watched the taillights of the car disappear into the darkness. Wisps of ground fog drifted from the woods across the rutted dirt road. She dug Mary's key out from under the mat and inserted it in the ignition, just in case.

She took the pistol's safety off for the same reason.

Then she settled in, as far from all the windows as she could get, and tried not to think that something was out there, in the darkness, watching her...with silver eyes.

Lick. Lick. Lick. Slowly he realized that he was on his back porch, nude in the dawn's light, licking his hand. His human hand. Something had scratched it, but that didn't explain the dried blood on his hands, his chest....

It was over. Again.

The first thing he did was throw up in the bushes. Blood. Then he staggered inside and showered. Blood stained his washcloth, but he could hide that. In his line of work, it would be easy to hide.

Emerging from the shower, he wondered if maybe he should stop hiding it. Maybe he should let them catch him. After all, he couldn't escape this cycle—could he?

A cycle. For the first time he wondered about the wolf that had cursed him. He couldn't remember it, but there must have been one. Did it have any control over him now?

His eyes narrowed. Another wolf. There had to be a connection, an out.

Another wolf.

CHAPTER FIVE

Disseminating Moon

A phone chirped nearby.

Sylvie frowned into her pillow, then winced against sunlight that was too bright for her still to be in bed. Then she remembered. She hadn't actually gone to bed until dawn had diluted the night to a pearly gray.

She'd kept her vigil in Mary's pickup truck, sure that at any moment a rabid lycanthrope would hurl itself against the windshield...but none had. She'd distracted herself by creating headlines for a news story. Local Woman Attacked by—what?

In barely fifteen minutes, a flashing of red and blue lights had announced the police. By the time she'd told the officers exactly what she and Brigit had seen—changing their ritual into a mere night out with the girls—Steve had arrived. He hadn't been happy. In fact, after his initial bone-crushing hug and a progress report on Mary, he hadn't spoken to Sylvie all the way home.

"I'll write the story before I go to bed," she'd volunteered, once they parked in silence outside the duplex. "Since the paper doesn't come out until tonight—"

"I don't care about the story!" Steve had bellowed.

"I care that my wife and my sister were out in the middle of nowhere—" He bit off the protest. For a moment brother and sister had just glared at one another.

Then he'd said, "Well, if you insist."

The phone chirped again. She propped herself up, and something crinkled beneath her elbow. Oh, yeah. After she'd sent her story to the *Sentinel*, via modem, she'd called up her computer's on-line encyclopedia and printed out everything she could find on werewolves. It hadn't been much. She needed to do some real research—and fast.

The phone.

She snatched it on its third ring, her lunge causing her hammock-style bed to sway. "Hello?"

"Hi. The bookstore's closed. Did I somehow miss Saturday completely?"

She closed her eyes and fell back on her pillows. Rand. She'd forgotten to call Rand! Now sunlight flooded her room, and the time for checking was well past. "What time is it?"

"Time is relative," the voice said, "but my watch says 10:45. Are you sick? If this is about our date tonight, you really don't have to miss work to get out of it. I'll try to control my suicidal tendencies. And, who knows? If I go through with them, I may *really* have a surprise at the haunted house. So you'd be doing me a favor."

"Normally I'm a morning person," she said carefully, "but I've had very little sleep, and this conversation is confusing me."

Rand shut up.

She had to check on Mary. And she definitely had to find out more about werewolves. Like how to keep Mary from turning into one. "Listen—I have to go into New Orleans to do some research today, and I'm not sure how late I'll be."

"Amazingly enough—" he'd adopted his salesman's voice, "—that is exactly what I was going to do. The New Orleans part, that is, without the research. I need to pick up some supplies. Would you like a ride and some company?"

Not if you nearly killed one of my best friends. But, disturbingly, she *would* like the company. All she had against Rand were suspicions and circumstantial evidence. In the light of day, she hardly believed she'd even seen a wolf last night, much less that it could have responded to his name.

In any case, she had another month until he was dangerous again.

Probably.

The Sylvie Peabody she'd once been—the one who'd boldly investigated ritual killings and poltergeist reports—came to the fore. What better way to investigate than to spend a day with a suspect? A very attractive suspect.

"Sylvie?"

"Yes," she said firmly. "Give me an hour to get ready, and we can go together."

"Going together—that's kinda like going steady, huh? Okay, okay, I'll give you a break," he told her cheerfully when she groaned. "Besides, I've never been accused of steadiness—or was that stability?"

"'Bye, Rand!" She hung up and flopped back in the bed.

It swayed slightly. She remembered how tired she was, but immediately made herself forget. Mary had been bitten by a werewolf—a *werewolf!* Did that mean she would become one?

"I won't let that happen," she decided, swinging her feet off the bed. If she had to read every damn book ever written about werewolves, she would find something.

If anything existed to be found.

An hour and a half later she was being driven to New Orleans in a hearse by a possible werewolf.

And she'd thought being a witch was unusual.

"Werewolves?" repeated Rand, when she admitted what she wanted to research. He looked darker than normal, possibly because he wore a crisp, long-sleeved black shirt against the surprising autumnal chill, possibly because of the grayness outside. They were crossing the Lake Pontchartrain Causeway—over twenty miles of bridge and water, with a rapidly clouding sky and nothing interesting but the company. Luckily the company was *very* interesting. The air around them surged and eddied with the now-familiar undercurrent of attraction and the scent of musk. "Hell, I'm a regular lycanthrophile. I know all about werewolves. Ask me something."

"How do you know about werewolves?" was her first question.

He risked glancing away from the bridge to flash her a surprised look; then the dimple reappeared. "Would you believe personal experience?" he teased.

"Possibly."

"I do like the gullible type," he mused to himself, not answering her question. His cheeks were shadowed, as if he hadn't shaved; his pale eyes looked tired. Had he been busy last night? "Werewolves. Well, shape-shifting is pretty common in legends. Without it, you've just got your normal folk hero. Then a startling metamorphosis occurs—and *grrr!*"

She wished he didn't growl so convincingly. She also wished the hearse didn't have such a smooth ride. Though she'd been wary of getting in at first, the interior appeared normal, and she'd long since relaxed.

She hid a yawn behind her hand. "So how does the curse happen?"

"You really don't know this?" So much for leading the witness.

She thought of Mary, released from the hospital and temporarily ensconced at Brie and Steve's. "You get bitten by a werewolf, right?"

"That's the traditional method, yes." With another assessing gray-eyed glance, Rand settled into his lecture. "Actually, there are two types of werewolves— voluntary and involuntary. The voluntary kind is probably based on psychos who got kicked out of their tribes when they had their buddies over for dinner.'' He paused, clearly waiting for her reaction, and she threw him a confused look. "Cannibals," he clarified cheerfully. "The exiles—lone wolves, you could say—gained a supernatural reputation. Then there's the involuntary lycanthropy connected to satanists and witches.''

She opened her eyes, only then aware that she'd momentarily closed them. Gray water stretched out on either side; they were still on the causeway. "Excuse me?''

"Just saying what the books say. Honest!'' He used his jeans-clad knee to steady the steering wheel while he made a cross with two fingers to hold her off; she stuck out her tongue.

He bit his lip and looked back at the bridge. She watched his tanned hands control the wheel; his muscled forearms were exposed by his rolled-up shirtsleeves. The undercurrents in the front seat tingled pleasurably. "There were even werewolf trials during the Inquisition that were pretty spooky," he said, almost sounding normal.

"The Burning Times," she agreed sadly, stretching against the seatback. So witches weren't the only ones who'd been hunted back then. She felt a momentary kinship with Rand—the enemy of my enemy is my friend, and all that. Then she reminded herself that he was as human as she was. "You said involuntary werewolves?''

"Are werewolves made or born?'' He leaned forward to assess the heavy clouds above them; there would be rain—but then again, this *was* Louisiana. "The answer, in fact, is both. Some stories tell about babies conceived or born on a certain day turning into wolves."

She closed her eyes again, letting his voice weave around her.

"Most legends focus on a person being bitten by another werewolf, so I guess it has something to do with the saliva. Nobody's mentioned the dangers of French-kissing a werewolf, though. Now that would make a good study...."

She listened to him as if from a great distance. After the first few raindrops splattered on the windshield, the beat of the wipers only put her farther under. That, and Rand's voice. She loved listening to it. He spoke with the skill of an actor, the rhythm of his words as full as their meaning.

He continued, saying, "I was thinking of doing some research on that very subject. Would you care to assist?" But even as she wondered what he was talking about, she forgot it completely.

Someone stroked her hair, feathering fingers through the light, shorter strands at the sides, gently massaging her scalp. With a little sigh she turned her head closer to the caress of callused fingers. They drifted off her hair and skimmed her cheek, electric on her skin.

She lifted her lids to meet gray eyes, very near hers; then she blinked awake. "We're not moving."

"We've arrived at Grandma's," explained Rand,

reluctantly trailing his fingers off her jaw and sitting back in the driver's seat. Some of his warmth retreated with him. That was when she recognized the sound of city traffic around them and saw that they were parallel-parked in front of the central library.

Pedestrians, hurrying by in the rain, threw the hearse worried looks. Even in a Southern city like New Orleans, sleepy by Yankee standards, people were in a rush. It was a contagious attitude; she, too, had work to do. "How long will your errands take?" she asked, half wishing Rand would reach out and stroke her hair again. Or maybe she could stroke his—the silky black ponytail looked particularly tempting.

"Two, three hours at the most. I could come get you at—" He glanced at his watch. "At four o'clock. As long as we're here, maybe we could find some charming little restaurant to eat at." His cheek dimpled with a smile. "I've found I like being charmed."

Outside, the pulse of the wet city called. Work to do, information to gather. She'd always been good at gathering information...even if she hadn't always used it wisely. But inside the car, with the rain drumming on the roof, they were separated from that world. Normally, her existence was a lonely thing, but he'd joined it.

"We could try the French Quarter," she suggested. Even witches and werewolves had to eat. Besides, she hadn't questioned him about last night.

"I thought the French used francs...." Rand began. Sylvie rolled her eyes and made a break for it. When she shut the door and stepped back under an over-hang, she got another good view of the hearse from the outside. She'd almost forgotten what she'd been riding in. That should not have happened.

From inside the black hearse Rand waved. Then he rejoined the New Orleans traffic.

With a single shiver, like a bird fluffing its feathers against the rain, she escaped into the city library.

Research—that was what had made her such a good reporter, what had gotten her bylines in Chicago and a job in Los Angeles. She'd never covered a psychic fair without knowing something about every psychic. She'd never investigated a haunted house without uncovering the property's complete history. She'd once helped the police catch a band of self-proclaimed satanists by researching ritual sacrifice until she found a pattern that matched the killings in question. Knowledge and objectivity—those were the keys.

She'd also done research into the cocaine underground to help her then-fiancé, Eddie, with a series of stories he was writing. Being in LA, that research had covered a lot of material. But she'd pieced together a series of patterns, names, places. Why hadn't she remembered them, once Eddie started mentioning those names and places in casual conversation?

Shaking away the memories, she found a directory and a computer catalog terminal and quickly buried herself in her current subject.

Rand was uncannily on target about the voluntary and involuntary werewolves, the cannibals and the werewolf trials. She found drawn-out, melodramatic accounts about some men named Verdun and Burgot who, in sixteenth-century France, had confessed to murdering children and "consorting with the devil" as werewolves. Their lycanthropy *did* sound like devil worship, and suspiciously like the sort of devil worship the old witch trials had "uncovered" through torture. "In other words, pure fiction," she muttered firmly, tracing a finger down the page. But she took notes anyway.

Then she paused, her pen hovering above her notebook. Another trial account told of a man named Gilles Garnier, condemned and burned for his lycanthropic killings. Gilles Garnier. Rand Garner.

Coincidence?

She flagged the page for photocopying and went on. It meant nothing, she told herself.

Then again, she'd thought the same thing about Eddie.

So her fiancé had become particularly alert, especially talkative? So he hadn't eaten much, slept much...weighed much. It meant nothing, she'd told herself then. She knew the symptoms of cocaine addiction. But she'd dismissed Eddie's behavior as hyperactivity.

She made a note in the margin—Check Garnier/ Garner—and tried not to feel like a traitor. Then she retreated into looking for a cure.

To her surprise, the silver-bullet theory was relatively new, based more on the legendary purity of silver than anything else—it supposedly killed vampires and witches, too. A lycanthrope might free himself by killing the wolf who had bitten him, another source suggested. And the people who spread werewolf stories had, it seemed, infinite faith in the power of the church to save them. Older "cures" included such things as having the wolf kneel on one spot for a hundred years, and addressing the wolf three times by his Christian name.

She cross-referenced the bibliographies she found in order to locate other volumes, then took more notes. She did a thorough periodical search. Finally stalled, she made photocopies of the most interesting information and bought a special library card so that she could check out four books. At least it was a start.

She glanced at the clock—it was still fifteen minutes before Rand would arrive—then checked her directory. There was a genealogy section. She could do some investigation into the Garner family, see if there were any connections to sixteenth-century France, if the name Garner derived from Garnier....

Not enough time. She would need more personal information. She could probably do it on her computer. All of which, translated, meant she didn't want to know.

Again.

Sylvie the Reporter shape-shifted back into Sylvie the bookseller, and she stared resentfully out the rain-streaked windows until the hearse pulled up in front.

"I meant to tell you," said Rand. "I enjoyed the article you wrote about me."

Sylvie's head snapped up from her contemplation of dessert, and she nearly spilled her tea. What? His grin showed his sharp canine teeth. The article about him?

Then she remembered—last week's *Sentinel* had run her story about the Deloup House's Halloween preparations. He probably hadn't read this week's paper yet.

"Thank you," she said, amazed at her own poise, and took a sweet bite of fried *beignet*. Powdered sugar dusted her lips, and she licked it off.

His gray eyes followed her tongue, and he seemed lost to all interest in his own food.

She shifted uncomfortably, and it wasn't because of the ladder-back chair.

They'd found a small café for dinner, hidden in a walled courtyard in the old French Quarter. Wrought-iron balconies overlooked the open-air patio—empty tonight, because of the wet—and added to its Old World atmosphere, the atmosphere of a world that could believe in werewolves.

Rand lifted his cup of dark, chicory-laced coffee to his sensuous lips. Despite his clowning over dinner and his flirtatious efforts to make her smile, he exuded a strong, tenacious sense of power.

She looked away from him. Over his shoulder, through open double doors, she caught a glimpse of glowing clouds, then the golden moon. People who didn't keep track of such things would think it was full tonight, instead of yesterday.

What had Rand been doing last night?

He followed her glance and said, "I think the rain's stopped. Shall we prowl?"

They walked slowly through the narrow, cobbled streets of the Quarter in the direction of Jackson Square. What had looked quaint by day somehow looked old and run-down in the gloom, and as they walked down the quieter side streets, their footsteps echoed off the closed, dark shops that loomed on both sides.

Distant rumbling signaled an approaching storm front, and the temperature dropped another degree or so. Rand, whistling with mock nonchalance, slid his hand around her waist, caressing her ribs through her oversize shirt and drawing her against him. If he *was* a monster, he was protecting her from any others that might be out there.

She studied his handsome profile from beneath the veil of her lashes. Surely her suspicions were little more than an overactive imagination. He couldn't truly be cursed!

Shouting sounded suddenly from down the block, and Rand's hold on her tightened, then relaxed as a young couple rounded the corner, waving their arms and yelling at each other. Two years of college French enabled Sylvie to do little more than recognize the language behind the Cajun accents.

"Uh-oh," murmured Rand. "She's tired of his carefree life as a...um...a jewel thief. She's telling him that her brother, an Interpol agent, has offered a reward." He paused in his "translation" while the couple stormed past. "Jacques, on the other hand, in-sists that the...um...the crown jewels of England would make a good retirement fund, and if Desirée would only—"

The woman screeched, and Sylvie spun around. The man had grasped her arm. The woman smacked it away and stalked away, gesturing.

Rand's hand, warm and firm against her back, eased her reluctantly forward.

"What if he's harassing her?" She twisted around again to watch the arguing couple, and Rand paused patiently beside her. If only her instincts were work-ing! "Do you think she even knows him?"

"In the Biblical sense, even," he said with a sigh, his voice dropping to a more honest note that indi-cated that his grasp of the language was better than hers. "He wants a divorce. She's saying she wants the house, but he messed up her credit." He squeezed her soothingly. "She's talking to him like he's a real wimp. I imagine she'll be safe."

"One more marriage turned statistic," she mut-tered, then realized two things. They'd reached the space and light of Jackson Square—and Rand spoke French.

"You understood them?" She tried not to let it sound like an accusation. She also tried not to think of sixteenth-century French werewolves.

"I spent some time in France as a kid," he ex-plained, whispering into her hair. As if on an after-thought, he turned his lips across her cheek and kissed her nose. She arched against his hard warmth and almost tipped her lips up to the pleasure of his, but fought the temptation.

From the iron-fenced garden that stood neatly between the spires of the St. Louis Cathedral and the Mississippi River, a statue of Andrew Jackson on horseback faced her. Her thoughts flew back to the arguing couple. Was it any wonder so many couples gave up? After the weight of the wedding, it all went downhill, straight into the legalities of name changes, credit, taxes and joint checking accounts. Maybe it was just as well she and Eddie hadn't made it to the altar. A mixed blessing...

They'd crossed the railroad tracks, and now they climbed the wide wooden stairs up the levee to the riverview walk. Below them stretched the incredible expanse of the Mississippi. On the far side of the river a tugboat pushed a barge. Nearer, one of the touristy riverboats paddled by. The high, curved Huey P. Long Bridge spanned the river to the south, already bright with glittering lights. But the river itself, deep and brown, dominated the scene. It had its own power, the power of age and space and a deceptively strong current that, like the sea, rarely gave up its dead. Which reminded her of her question. She'd promised herself she would ask. She had to know.

"So what did you do last night?" She hoped the words came out casually. He wrapped both arms around her against the drizzle that had begun to mist down on them.

"I was guarding the house," he explained softly, his chicory-scented breath hot on her ear. Before she could ask why, he added, "I thought I saw someone suspicious lurking around."

The werewolf! But her questions—what time, where, what did the trespasser look like—stopped in her throat as if an invisible hand had silenced her.

He was lying.

He leaned nearer and touched her lips with his, but her roiling suspicions battled the electricity of the kiss. She could have dismissed a mere suspicion; she'd been doing it all day! But this was more than suspicion. This was the stuff that kept people from getting onto doomed airplanes, that signaled wives about philandering husbands, that made mothers check on their children just in time.

She recognized instinct when she felt it.

After such a long absence, why did it have to kick in now, with this tidbit about him? But it had, and she couldn't ignore it. Rand was lying to her, just as Eddie had lied to her, and she suddenly couldn't bear the ache in her chest.

"Are you all right?" he asked, when she didn't respond to his kiss.

"I'm cold." It took no effort to lie. That was one benefit of her usual reserve. "We should head back."

"You sure—" he began, but she'd already turned out of the warmth of his arms and started for the stairs, and he followed.

For most of the walk back through the cobbled dampness of the Quarter, he remained a breath behind her, his presence looming, his footsteps echoing separately from hers. The darkness lightened as they approached the hearse. They'd parked near enough to Bourbon Street to hear the scream of a clarinet, the howl of a trumpet. One block down, people partied and drank and worried not at all.

When Rand circled her to unlock the shiny black door, he looked at her with suspicion...and hunger.

She didn't think he was protecting her anymore.

If she broke away, ran... But she couldn't run from what frightened her without leaving what fascinated her.

She climbed into the hearse.

The drive north toward Stagwater grew more tense by the mile. The storm hit, slapping wind and rain across the freeway so hard that traffic slowed to a snarl. The outside violence only emphasized the silence within. After fifteen minutes of half-blind stop-and-go, Rand finally growled something about taking the long way around the lake and avoiding the causeway altogether.

"Fine," she said, although she knew it would take twice as long.

He missed the eight-mile bridge to neighboring Slidell, but at least the two-lane road around the lake had less traffic. Through lulls in the rain she caught glimpses of fishing-boat masts, and she lost track of how many drawbridges they crossed. Old rock and roll played on the radio, so she didn't have to make conversation. But this wasn't like the drive into New Orleans. Now she was all too aware of riding in a hearse. Boxes and cartons and what looked like giant paint cans that would never have fit in the Volkswagen filled the back. She couldn't fault his choice of vehicles there.

But when the hearse began to buck and sputter, she *did*. Rand fought it, giving the engine more gas, downshifting, but it only shuddered again. Dividing his attention between both mirrors, growling beneath his breath, he managed to ease the hearse onto the shoulder of the road before all the lights on the dashboard flashed red in a dramatic stall.

"Your timing," he muttered sweetly to it, "stinks." And he snapped off the radio and sat stiffly back.

Rain drummed hard on the roof and windshield. Breathe in the positive energy, breathe out the negative energy, she told herself. This wasn't a disaster, just a breakdown—right?

"What do you think is wrong?" she asked, if only to break the silence between them.

He drew a strained breath. "It won't go." Before she could respond, he lifted a hand for patience and undid his seat belt. "I have a list of possible suspects. Wait here."

"You're going out in that?" She could hardly see out for the water washing down the windows.

"I just want to check something," he assured her, opening the door. Immediately the wind grabbed it and yanked it open. Rain blew in, splashing her, while he dived out. When he did shut the door, the resulting silence echoed. She tried to watch him move to the front of the car and pop the hood, but could only discern a water-warped shadow in the headlights.

They'd broken down in the middle of nowhere? If her parents had still been alive and waiting for her to make it home by curfew, they never would have bought it. If he'd run out of gas, *she* wouldn't buy it, either!

A face loomed at her window. She recoiled, and its owner tapped on the glass. Rand. Expelling a cautious sigh of relief, she cracked the window. Rain flew in. In the darkness she could make out dripping hair and eyes squinted against the wet.

"Try to start the engine," he called.

Nodding, she unfastened her belt to slide across the seat onto the driver's side. When she turned the key, the motor cranked, sputtered, caught. Then, with a hacking shudder, it died.

Just like in a horror movie.

She tried it again, giving it more gas. It caught, then immediately began to buck. She stayed on the gas, pumping it, willing the engine to go, to go, to—

The door beside her swung open with a blast of rain. "You'll flood it," called Rand, even as she jumped back from his sudden appearance. The engine coughed and died. Giving her another assessing look, he climbed into the seat she'd vacated and pulled the door shut. His shirt sagged in wet folds, clinging to the planes of his chest, his back, his shoulders. His hair had come loose and now dripped down the sides of his face and neck. "I think it's the distributor cap, but it doesn't look cracked, only wet," he said, and made a face. "Especially now. We'll just have to wait it out."

"How long will that take?"

"We can try it again in fifteen minutes. I guess until then…"

She shuddered—he had to be freezing—and he folded his wet arms. "Too much caffeine, Syl?"

The direct attack caught her off guard. "What?"

"Credit me with a little imagination. You're thinking I lured you out here and arranged some hokey breakdown."

"I didn't say—"

"But you're thinking it. You've been jumping at shadows all day. What's wrong?"

Distant, careful. He shouldn't have been able to see behind the calm facade! "Nothing."

He stared out the window and swiped wet strands of hair back from his face. Then he looked back at her, his pale eyes serious. "You know, when I first saw you, I thought, now there's a woman who's really together. You were cool about the witch books, you were casual about the haunted house, nothing ruffled your feathers. Now, all at once, you're ruffled. Why?"

The words came out before she'd thought them through. "I think there's a werewolf in Stagwater."

The foot or so of space between them crackled, tension mounting in the silence. Then Rand, shifting to get more comfortable, said, "There's no such thing as werewolves."

"You said the same thing about witches," she reminded him.

"And you whipped out your membership card and

proved me wrong. What are you going to do now—turn into a wolf?''

''No. Are you?'' The challenge hung between them. It wouldn't take much. His narrowed, pale eyes already looked lupine, feral in his frustration. When he smiled, his bared teeth completed the picture.

He loomed closer; she drew back. ''The idea has its merits,'' he growled—and in one motion, too fluid to be a lunge, he pressed her back against her door and covered her mouth with his own.

CHAPTER SIX

Waning Moon

For a moment her world stilled—the drop in air pressure before a tornado—and in that moment Rand's lips devoured hers hungrily. He worked his fingers into her hair, cushioning her head from the cold, hard window and its drumroll of windblown rain, while his tongue darted teasingly along the corner of her mouth. As if she were taking part in a relaxation exercise out of control, she felt herself going limp—legs, torso, arms, even her usually stiff neck, her usually careful face. The hearse's rooftop shuddered under pelting, angry rain, but his damp, warm body covered and protected her.

The tingling warmth that began to spark into life deep within her did not recede when, with a last nibble at her lower lip, he pulled back.

He made no apologies, didn't look like a man who would apologize. His hunger fueled his eyes from the shadows of loose, dripping hair. Feral, wild, dangerous—but pausing.

Giving her a chance to retreat.

The wind beat at the hearse, shaking it.

She reached upward, clasped him by the scruff of his neck and pulled him back to her.

His warmth, like a fur coverlet, cocooned her now. Her shields dropped and allowed his very essence to wrap itself around her and through her. His foot scraped on the floor mat for purchase as he eased her away from the door that braced her, pulled her down onto the vinyl seat, then lay over her again. Legs entwined with legs; arms embraced.

She met his mouth eagerly, her own energy meeting his, encircling him. They kissed, licking and nipping, worrying each other's mouths, while their combined heat mixed and produced desire. She felt its charge through her weakened limbs, realized her strength to move beneath him.

"Oh, Lord," he panted during a momentary lull.

Through the veil of her lashes, she saw his teeth—and his dimple.

When he scattered more kisses across her mouth, she arched her back, pressing the growing ache of her need closer to the jeans-clad hardness of his own. Cerebral Sylvie, aloof Sylvie, floated indifferently upward, leaving physical Sylvie to her pleasures. Good…oh, so good.…

He fumbled at her shirt buttons, clawing the starched yellow cotton open, nibbling along her throat, around her collarbone, past the pentagram between her breasts. His hands burrowed beneath her shirt, their callused roughness stroking the soft skin on her spine, unclasping her bra. He lifted her to him, raising her breasts closer to his roaming mouth. Nibbles became licks, encircling, arousing. She heard quiet little whimpers—hers? his?—and found power beyond the whirlwind of sensation to grasp his waterlogged shirt and yank it loose from his stiff, restricting jeans. There! His own skin was hot, his ribs surging beneath her hands with the force of his breath. She stroked up them, spread her fingers through the hair that shadowed his chest. He moved his attention upward, slid his rough cheek over hers, chewed on her ear. His chest came down on hers, trapping her hands against him, tickling her bare breasts beyond endurance. He moved atop her, and she writhed beneath him. Working one knee between his, she caught one of his thighs between hers. It helped—and made it worse. Did she imagine it, or was there a pulsating glow surrounding them, just past sight? The energy they were generating was probably in Technicolor!

His hair brushed her cheek, his teeth worked her earlobe, his breath burned against her temple. He was lean and sure atop her; she allowed it. Animal? Wolf? It didn't matter—whatever he was, she needed him. Her soul cried for him. She turned her head and chewed lightly on the corner of his mouth in some instinctual show of submission.

He paused, panting, crouched above her.

She caught the waistband of his jeans, fighting wet denim to unbutton them. He arched with pleasure and skimmed one hand down to her own jeans—and dropped protectively atop her when a glare of light and a sharp rapping broke them from their spell.

Confusion buffeted her overloaded senses. She was almost sure she heard him whimper into her neck. The cerebral, aloof Sylvie snapped back into control, silently demanding an explanation, and another glare of light, dappled with rainwater, flashed past. Rand turned his face away from it, an animal caught in headlights.

Rap, rap, rap. "Hey! You folks got any reason to be parked here?"

"The police!" she breathed.

"He couldn't see anything," Rand assured her, his voice rough, and he pushed himself up enough to let her pull her shirt closed. "Don't worry—he couldn't see anything."

A few more minutes, though, and he sure would have gotten a show!

When she was decent, he pulled himself stiffly over into the driver's seat. She huddled back against the passenger door, where she'd been before all this started, and leaned her flushed cheek against the cold glass. She hoped it would ease some of the heat that still roiled, unfulfilled, through her.

Cool, wet air flowed over her when Rand cranked his own window down. "Can I help you, Officer?"

"May I see your license and registration, son?" The raincoat-clad state trooper who leaned near the window, rain pattering on his dark blue Smoky the Bear hat, seemed wary, but hardly hostile.

Of course he was wary. They were in a hearse.

Rand closed his eyes momentarily as he dug out his wallet, as if in pain. The trooper took his time examining the ID. "South Carolina," he mused finally. "What are you doin' round these parts?"

There was a significant pause, during which Rand

cut his eyes toward her. They sparkled mischievously. She bit her lip. He cleared his throat. "I live here now."

"You'll need to be gettin' a Louisiana license," the trooper drawled, and flashed his oversize light past Rand, at her. "Ma'am, are you all right?"

She nodded, squinting in the glare. "Yes. Thank you. The car wouldn't start." Her words sounded cool and assured, but for a millisecond the trooper's face was transposed on an officer's from last night—"*You sure you didn't see the attacker's face?*"—then again with the officer who had come to question her about Eddie, back in LA. *"When did you last see your fiancé alive, miss?"*

"Why don't we just give her a listen?" the trooper suggested, and Rand obediently turned the ignition key.

The engine growled to life. Rand dropped his forehead against the steering wheel and shook his head at the irony of life in general.

The state trooper was beginning to look suspicious. "Well, folks, looks like it's runnin' fine now. Maybe y'all ought to be headin' on home. Isn't safe in these parts during a full moon, lately. Seems to be some kinda psycho runnin' 'bout, north of the lake."

"The moon was full *last* night," Rand pointed out, his voice less muffled as he raised his head.

"It looked full enough afore the rain hit." The trooper tapped the brim of his dripping hat and retreated to the dark blue patrol car parked behind them. Rand shuddered off the confrontation like a dog shaking off water and pulled back onto the road. The rain, while still steady, had lessened.

While he seemed to be concentrating on the wet road revealed by their headlights, she discreetly fastened the rest of her shirt buttons. What had just happened back there?

"Well," he said finally, "at least we aren't fighting anymore."

Had they been fighting? She flushed at the memory. They'd almost had sex in the front seat of a hearse was what had happened. And it had almost been terrific.

And yes, he might be a werewolf—but not tonight.

"Are you all right?" He seemed to ask her that a lot. "I'm sorry about what happened. With the cop, I mean. I'm not sorry…" He shrugged, cut his eyes in her direction. "You're really something, Sylvie Peabody. I have absolutely no idea what the hell is going on between us, but when it does, I'm not at all sorry."

When he held out a hand, she gave him hers, glad of the affection that flowed into her from his closing fingers. She should say she wasn't sorry, either. And she wasn't. Yet. But, oh, she could end up being very, very sorry. "Whatever's happening, it's sure happening quickly," she said instead.

He chewed his lip, then said, "I can try to keep my animal tendencies to myself. You're welcome to slap me on the nose if I get out of hand."

But when she was with him, in his arms, she wanted to be an animal, too. It wasn't that at all.…

"Sylvie?" he prompted. "Talk to me. Please."

"I wish I could trust you!" Stupid thing to say—now he would reassure her that she could. And she still wouldn't know for sure. "I don't mean the…"

"Sparking?" he offered cheerfully. "Necking? 'Cept there were more than necks involved. Spooning? Bundling?"

"Bundling?"

"Old World term—real big a few hundred years ago. So you're okay with that…. That's always a plus. What don't you trust?"

"Secrets."

The word hung between them. His next glance was assessing. "Been consulting the ol' crystal ball, Syl?"

"Should I?"

"Not unless you're ready to handle what you see." His voice was no longer teasing.

"What would I see?" she asked softly, reluctantly.

They drove almost another mile, silence broken only by the beat of the windshield wipers, before Rand said, "Nothing important."

Never before had the decision to invite a man in or not been so complicated.

"Here we are, *mademoiselle,*" he announced, pulling to a stop by the curb behind her Pinto and killing the engine. "Let me get your door." And he got out—the rain had given up, for the moment—and came around the front of the hearse, past the headlights. He looked a little wild; his hair was still down, turning shaggy as it dried. That reminded her of how it had gotten down in the first place. Desire stirred, like unsated hunger at the smell of food. His smooth, controlled stride tempted her; his near-dry jeans gave new meaning to the term *shrink to fit*. When he opened her door and his strong fingers grasped her hand to help her out, she found herself standing close in front of him—too close.

"I imagine 'Let's do it again sometime' is the wrong phrase to use here," he said softly. "Especially until we check schedules with the nice policeman." Despite the lows of the evening, he was smiling. Oh, yes, she wanted to invite him in. Suspicions, worries, doubts—all of those merely got in the way. Suspicions were mere psychological babble compared to the reality of physical attraction.

"Maybe we can leave him out?" she suggested equally softly, and leaned forward, into him. She felt a smile soften her lips when his hands slid possessively around her waist. She was getting good at smiles.

"You sure it won't hurt his feelings?" He dipped his head nearer hers, touched noses with her.

"Do you care?"

"Uhn—" He brushed her lips with a restrained little kiss, the sort of kiss to make her insides flutter. "However," he added as he inhaled, "I do care about *you*. Maybe it's not so wise, in light of this trust thing.... Maybe we should give ourselves a little more time." He spoke so tenderly that it took her a minute to realize he was saying no.

Okay, she told herself firmly, mentally gritting her

teeth. She had to respect that. But even though she didn't speak, her eyes must have. He said, "I lost control in the car earlier. I do that sometimes. Usually it doesn't turn out so well. But, Syl…"

She tipped her head the fraction needed to touch her own lips to his. Electricity. His hands remained locked behind her waist, holding her intimately against him. "But?"

"But when we do get together, I don't want anything between us," he answered. "Not distrust, not doubt, not uncertainty."

"But—" He silenced her with another kiss, and her protest floated away, dissolving into the humid, fertile night around them. Then a light came on from the direction of the duplex.

"Uh-oh," he muttered, his lips deserting hers. "Dad's waiting up."

She glanced over her shoulder and saw Steve and Brie's door opening. "No, Mom," she told him with a groan.

He followed her gaze to see Brie emerge onto the porch, curly hair catching the front light in fiery sparks. "That's your *mom?*"

"Might as well be." Since it looked as if Brie was approaching anyway—retiring flower that she was— Sylvie waved. "Hello, Brigit. Why don't you join us? And Mary!" she added at a glimpse of blond hair in the doorway. "I want you to meet someone."

"Is this wise?" questioned Rand, loosening his hold on her waist and leaning discreetly back from her.

"Don't worry, they're just my circlemates."

"Your—*they're witches, too?*"

By now, Brie's stride had carried her across the lawn and to the sidewalk. "Hello," she said, holding out her hand challengingly. "You must be Rand Garner."

"Must I?" But he accepted the hand and shook it.

"Rand, this is Brigit Peabody and Mary Deveraux." Sylvie noticed only then that Mary, who had arrived quietly in Brie's wake, was still hanging back. Neither she nor Rand initiated a handshake—but then, Mary's bandaged arm hung in a sling.

"Sylvie, we've got to talk," Brie said. "Nice meeting you, Rand."

"Brigit!" Sylvie noted thankfully that he didn't look at all insulted; in fact, his good-natured smirk played with the idea that he'd often been dismissed. But she felt the insult for him. "I'll be in in a minute, thank you."

"It's important," said Brie.

Sylvie frowned down at her, but Brie didn't budge. Then Mary, too, said, "It's important." But she said it more softly, and suddenly Sylvie thought maybe it was true. She glanced back at Rand, torn.

"I have to be going anyway," he assured her. "Besides, I sense tar and feathers in the future, and that's just not my look."

"Rand—"

He kissed her forehead and backed away, his hands spread. "I know where you live now," he warned her with a grin.

"Mmm... Witches don't take kindly to trespassers. Remember your fairy tales." She collected her library books while he climbed into the driver's seat, where, from the shadows, he blew a kiss to her. "But consider yourself invited," she added softly, and waved before shutting the door. Then he was pulling away. Suddenly chilly, she turned to her friends. "This had better be good."

"Your shirt is buttoned wrong," Brie noted.

Mary covered her mouth with her good hand. "Oh, Sylvie! You didn't!"

"That's none of your business." Sylvie stalked toward her own door, but Brie cut her off, leaping onto the porch and pressing herself back against the door's stained-glass panels. Her smoky blue eyes flared with amazement. "In a hearse?"

Sylvie expelled an exaggerated sigh. "I'm not in a good mood, Brie."

"He was that bad, huh?" Her sister-in-law knew when to dodge, and now she did so, laughing an apology. "I'm sorry, I'm sorry, I'm sorry! Just kidding!"

Mary said, "It's not funny," and Brie stopped laughing. The small blonde looked tired and frail, Sylvie realized, and not just because of the sling. "You've got to come see what I found." If Brie had asked at that point, she might well have refused. But Mary...

"Okay," she agreed, turning to follow the women into Brie's place. "But it better be good."

"That," warned Brie, "depends upon your definition of the word *good*."

* * *

Mary's tarot deck sat on Brie's homespun table-cloth. "Remember how last week I put away the last four cards without looking at them?" Mary prompted, sinking into an antique chair. "I laid them on top of the deck, to check them later. Then I didn't get around to it—maybe I didn't want to. But today I decided I'd better confront them. And look what came up as the current situation card." With her good hand, she flipped up the picture of a brown-haired woman, sword in hand. The Queen of Swords. Sylvie.

"But it couldn't be there," Sylvie argued, lowering herself into another chair. "It had already come up."

Brie said, "No kidding."

"I know it already came up," said Mary patiently. "That's why I'm so confused—somehow, the cards got mixed. In any case, look at what they're saying." She turned the card that would symbolize Sylvie's surroundings. The Moon—deceit, illusion, change-ability. The dog and the wolf still mirrored each other.

The next card Mary flipped showed a man with a chalice in his hands. "The King of Cups," Sylvie muttered, knowing already that it symbolized Rand. "What does that position represent again?"

"What you either want, or fear," said Mary, meeting her eyes steadily. "Or both." They jumped when Romeow landed on the table to see what they were doing. Brie scooped the fluffy pumpkin-colored cat into her arms and kissed the top of his head, glancing nervously toward the front door in case Steve came home and caught them.

The outcome card lay unturned, its Celtic design

slightly smudged, its edges worn from use. When Mary didn't move to turn it, Sylvie did. A skeleton, dressed in black, rode a black horse over prone bodies.

Death.

"Correct me if I'm wrong," Sylvie said with careful calm, "but this card does not always mean actual death, right?"

"It usually shows endings and beginnings." Mary lifted her hazel eyes. "But it can also mean death. Please stay away from this man, Sylvie."

She'd felt so safe with him. They'd been so good together. "You have no proof."

Brie said, "We aren't exactly the sort of people who need proof, kid. I'm no psychic, but even I think he's hiding something."

"And I should just ask him what it is? People don't keep secrets just because they haven't been asked! They keep secrets because they don't intend for anyone to find out, and if someone finds out, they lie!" She'd learned that the hard way, with Eddie.

"So be careful of him until you do find out," persisted Mary.

"You're only saying that because you're scared."

"Yes! I *am* scared!" Mary put her cards back in their box, awkward because of being one-handed. "Of course I am. Think about it—don't you know what it means if he really is a werewolf? What it means to me?"

A flash of white canines, narrowed, lupine eyes.

Dimples. "He's too nice to be a werewolf," Sylvie insisted.

Brie put a comforting hand on her shoulder. "Being mean is not necessarily a prerequisite, kid."

Mary nodded, dead serious. "Just look at me."

Be careful of him until you do find out.

Sylvie hated the concept of proof. To someone who lived by her intuition, evidence merely iced the cake. Proof convinced skeptics of a truth that was already obvious to anyone with an ounce of instinct.

Which she no longer had.

She'd done a story on a women's shelter several years ago, in Chicago. How many "perfect" men had turned out to be abusers or rapists—or drug addicts? Some werewolf stories didn't need full moons, and some women's instincts led them into their own horror stories.

So she spent all of Sunday and most of Monday morning at UnderCover, trying to gather information impersonally. The security she felt with Rand, and the attraction, had to be put aside for her investigation to work. Knowledge *and* objectivity.

Objectively she knew that Rand had been busy on the night of the full moon and that he was new in town. So much for proof. She didn't even know he'd lied—objectively speaking.

Recognizing a Werewolf, she'd written atop one sheet of paper, but she'd made few notes. Only one of her books suggested a werewolf might appear hairier or toothier than a normal person. That author didn't explain, though, why family members wouldn't notice that kind of change. *Too bad he's not a vampire,* she'd written in disgust. At least vampires showed consistent signs—no reflection, avoiding garlic, vaporizing in direct sunlight. Werewolves only became werewolves on the night of the full moon.

Which could make them as hard to sense, the rest of the time, as they were to spot.

She tried not to think about that. Instead, she took heart from another sheet of notepaper. *Women Werewolves,* she'd titled it—with absolutely nothing beneath. She couldn't find a single incident in legend or history of a female lycanthrope. Was it because the chroniclers of times past had not been able to imagine a woman with that kind of power? Or was there a chance that women were immune?

Hopeful news for Mary.

She tried to feel happier about it.

At noon she put up her Out to Lunch sign and drove her library books to Thomas Prints. This would work much better if she could write in the margins and merely highlight the important stuff. "I won't use this for personal gain," she promised Don as he accepted the books from her and turned to use the machine behind the counter. He didn't protest. Don had been a quiet, easygoing man even before his wife's death. Nowadays he was so melancholy, he probably wouldn't protest a Stagwater Nudist Day—and him the son of a preacher.

Leaning against a glass case full of office supplies, lulled by the chugging of the photocopier and the smell of paper and dry ink, she frowned at that thought. Don's wife hadn't merely died—she'd been killed by wild dogs, three months ago.

What if those hadn't been ordinary dogs?

Studying the small, balding man who was flipping to her next bookmark, she began to put her clues together. Rand had only been in town a few weeks before poor Dennis Gareaux's death, right? So if Mrs. Thomas had also been killed by the werewolf, Rand had to be innocent!

Proof!

"You want just this page, Miss Sylvie, or the whole chapter?" Don asked now, and she made herself act casual.

"The whole chapter, if you're allowed to do that."

"I'll do it." And he started copying again.

She glanced around the counter until she spotted a desk calendar—Compliments of Thomas Prints—and traced the days back. This was early September, and the barley moon had been last Friday. A month before, early August, had been the wort moon. That had been the night Dennis Gareaux was killed. And before that... But when she traced a month back to the mead moon, her finger paused uncertainly.

Something didn't seem right.

Reluctantly she allowed her finger to backtrack two more weeks to the date of the summer solstice, in June. Their Midsummer rites had been dampened by the recent death of Mrs. Thomas, almost two weeks past the full moon.

Damn. For a minute she'd thought she scented

something legitimate. That was what came of a psi potato following her gut feelings.

"Miss Sylvie?" Don stood in front of her; her copies and library books lay neatly on the counter. "That'll be $6.49. Will that be on your account at UnderCover, or do you want to handle it now?" The poor man had lost his wife, and here she stood trying to build a werewolf story around it. Now that was *desperate!*

Because you don't want it to be Rand, Miss Objectivity.

"I'll pay now," she murmured, angry at herself for jumping at shadows. The only solution was to act impersonally and learn something. And, damn it, for better or worse, that was what she planned to do.

"Sylvie Peabody?" repeated the gruff male voice over the phone. "It's really you? Lord and Lady, I thought you'd vanished off the edge of the world!"

"Louisiana," she clarified. "But you can see the edge of the world from here."

"I haven't talked to you since—oh." James Radcliff was a Druidic high priest who just happened to work for the Los Angeles district attorney's office. Or maybe it was the other way around, and he just happened to be a high priest. In any case, he had helped her piece together the real story of what had happened the night Eddie died.

Still, she should have kept in touch…. At least a card at Yule.

"That's okay, Jimmy. I always meant to let you know where I'd gone, but…"

"Hey, you're a free agent, sunshine. Owe nobody—that's the secret. So what can I do for you?"

She spun at the sound of bells on her shop door, then caught her breath. Just some teenage girls, out of school for the day. Only then did she realize she'd been afraid it was Rand, afraid he would catch her. She stood a little straighter, challenging those fears. "I'd like you to run a check on someone, Jimmy."

"You working on a story? 'Cause, on the record, I don't pass out people's backgrounds for publication."

"Completely off the record, Jimbo. I want to know if this person has had any brushes with the law, particularly relating to violent crimes. Can you do that for me?"

"I'm not supposed to, but there are rules and then there are rules. Is he in California?"

She thought back to the night the state trooper checked Rand's license. "I think his previous residence is South Carolina."

"A challenge! And what's the name?"

Again she glanced across the store, as if somebody there would hear, would tell. The teenagers were clustered in front of the romance section, comparing passages, oblivious to her. Now or never, Peabody. "His name is Rand Garner," she made herself say. "About five foot eleven, long black hair—not going gray, but a slate kind of black." Lean, graceful, strong, sexy as sin…

"Length can change. Is the color natural?"

"I think so. Gray eyes. He's currently doing special effects on a haunted house—his background should reflect that." And he may turn into a wolf on a regular basis. That reminded her of something. "If it helps, the occurrences I'm interested in would take place on the full moon."

"And yet you're worried about his background. This guy wouldn't be a satanist, would he?"

"Not exactly." The bell on the door jingled again—Miss Amanda, in for more mysteries. "Listen, Jimmy, I've got to go. If you find anything, please let me know as soon as possible. I'll owe you."

"What I give, I give freely. I do need one thing from you though, sunshine."

She hated to ask. Making contact with Los Angeles made her nervous—and not just because of Eddie. She'd never been completely comfortable there. "What?"

"Your phone number. Or are you afraid to hear what I might have to say?"

"That hasn't stopped us before, has it?" But she gave him her work number. Her hand was shaking when she hung up.

She was doing the practical thing, looking for proof. If she was lucky, there would be nothing to find, and then she could confess and apologize to Rand. And if there was something, she should know about it.

So why did she feel so guilty?

* * *

It made sense.

He was a werewolf, an abomination, because of another abomination. There were two of them. Didn't the paper say that a girl had been attacked on the same night a man disappeared? Two attacks, two werewolves.

If he couldn't stop himself—and, wretch that he was, he couldn't—there was something he could do. He could find the other werewolf, go to him, try to discover some way to break the link and lift the curse.

Perhaps. *With that one word, he tried to curb his welling hope that he could live a normal, loving life.* Perhaps.

Either way, he had to find the monster. And he had a good idea where to look....

CHAPTER SEVEN

Crescent Moon

"**I** vant to bite your neck! Blagh! Blagh!"

Sylvie spun in surprise—Rand had entered the bookstore silently again—and ducked away from his black-caped swoop toward her throat. Stymied, he snapped his fingers in defeat and grinned at her, elongated canine teeth gleaming dangerously.

"What are you doing here?" she asked, and immediately regretted it. She tried not to glance guiltily at the counter, which hid the phone. It had been three days since she'd called Jimmy—and nearly a week since she'd last seen Rand. The helpless waiting was beginning to wear on her.

He narrowed his lupine eyes. They were too light for the undead, she thought, and his handsome features were too pleasant, even in the overcast daylight that struggled through UnderCover's front windows. No, Rand just wasn't vampire material. Perhaps he really *could* be a werewolf, though. In his usual good mood, he had that scampish, easy attitude she equated with dogs, and in his darker moments he could seem as dangerous as any alpha male defending its territory.

Which Rand would she be facing if he learned she was investigating him?

He folded his arms so that the black cape flowed back from his elbows like bat wings—Dracula on a down day. "I hoped to interest you in a bite," he told her with a leer. The *s* in *interest* hissed a little.

"Or an overbite?" she prompted in a belated effort to sound casual.

"Pretty neat, huh? They're real—well, made out of the same stuff dentures are made of, so real enough. They fit over my own teeth. Lenny looks great in his. You'll have to see him."

She gathered the stack of paperbacks she'd been shelving on his arrival and paused with them balanced on her hip, willing the phone not to ring. "Pretty neat," she agreed, and he swooped in for a kiss.

The wings of his cape enveloped her as his lips captured hers. She sank guiltily into the sensation, the thrill of unwise intimacy—then jerked back from the prick of one of his fangs. Reality, she supposed, and tried to fight back the sense that it had been an omen. She didn't believe in bad omens.

"Sorry." He traced the scratch with his finger, wincing, then leaned back and popped off both fake teeth. Compared to the vampire look, his own normally sharp canines appeared quite human. He kissed her injury more carefully—tasting her blood?

"So what are you doing here?" she repeated, this time on purpose. "Not that I'm not glad to see you...."

"Interesting you in a bite," he insisted, but he backed away, raising his hands before she could throw something at him. "I brought pizza." With a flare of his cape and a jingling of bells, he swooped from the store to his hearse outside.

She didn't even have time to cry, "Wait!"

Great. He'd brought lunch here, to the bookstore. She'd thought she would know something concrete before seeing him—or deciding not to see him—again. Instead, she was suddenly running the risk of his being here while he learned whatever dark truths Jimmy might unearth. Or while he learned she'd run an unethical background check on an innocent man. She should beg off, somehow duck out of this until she knew more.

He reentered, balancing a pizza box and a paper bag. "Your repast, *mademoiselle,*" he said, placing the food on the counter and joining her on the dais behind it. He paused momentarily, head cocked, as he studied her single wooden stool. "Hmm...a minor logistical problem."

Now or never. "Actually, Rand, I—" Her words tumbled out, catching his surprised attention. "I wasn't expecting you to come by, and—" But she couldn't finish the excuse. The smell of pizza tempted her...as did his expectant gray gaze.

"You're not hungry," he guessed.

Little did he know.

She kicked off her sandals, hiked herself onto the counter and smoothed her creamy peasant skirt down, leaving the stool for him. *Please, Jimmy,* she willed at the telephone on the shelf beneath her. *Please don't call now.*

Rand extracted two large cups and a pile of napkins

from the bag and opened the pizza box, releasing a cloud of spicy steam. He had to throw his cape back over his shoulders to protect it from tomato sauce.

She had to ask. "You wore that getup into Pizza Palace?"

"Sure. It wasn't half as much fun as the blood bank, though. 'Give me three pints, B negative!' Actually," he explained, "I've got nameplates on the hearse—'Haunted Deloup House, Open October.' That's not even a month away, you know." He served her a cheesy wedge of pizza, then separated one for himself. "I'm going to be pretty busy from now until November. But I still want to see you. In fact..." Putting down his napkin, he backed up a step and looked at her for a long moment. She got the fluttery feeling that maybe he *could* see her—*her,* not just the cool mask she wore.

Could he see the suspicion, then? Could he see the guilt?

"There," he said, straddling the stool again and leaning one elbow on the counter beside her thigh. His smile was endearing. "That should last me a day or so." And he bit into his pizza.

She poked him in the thigh with a bare foot. "You are a very strange man."

"Yeah," he agreed cheerfully, and took a long draw of his cola. "But you're a witch—that evens us out."

"Does that bother you?" She picked up a straw wrapper to twist around her finger. "Me being a witch?"

His eyes sparkled up at her. "Nope. As long as you don't mind about me."

Her heartbeat slowed with suspicion. Not more trouble. Not yet. "What about you?"

He looked quickly away. "What? Oh, nothing. Nothing at all. Did I say something? Have some pizza." Only when he offered her another wedge did she note the teasing dimples; this time she nudged him in the ribs. He caught her ankle, and electricity flowed up her leg at his touch.

"You're awful," she told him in a chiding tone.

"You've barely tried me." His return fairly sizzled between them; then he stroked her captured foot and let her go.

She released a breath, only then realizing that she'd been holding it. She shouldn't let him be here at all, much less be feeling the attraction she felt…but some things were beyond intellect, and this was one of them.

While they finished eating he told her about his work on the haunted house. He and Terry—his long-time assistant—and even Lenny were working long hours, he explained, but the place was really coming together. She enjoyed watching him, listening to him, long after the pizza and colas were gone. Her ease with him, her undeniable attraction to him, the soft way his energy mingled with hers…all of those things comprised more than companionship.

He obviously trusted her. Again the fact that she was investigating him pressed down on her. If he was innocent, she didn't deserve him.

And if he wasn't—?

Then he ended, "So I'd really like it if you could come by in a few nights and look at it."

She tried not to look startled. "The house?"

"You could give me some ideas about the witch room—not that I can promise to change it—and we could have dinner. Terry convinced me not to go with gory in the dining room, so it's actually very elegant. When there aren't decapitated zombies wandering through, that is. And I'll give them the night off."

She hadn't heard from Los Angeles yet—but she still might.

"It might be my last free night in some time," he added—and just as she'd sensed his lie that night in the French Quarter, she knew that now he was telling the truth. His busy season was coming up, and he wanted to see her. Nothing wrong with that. She very much wanted to see him, too.

As he'd put it once, she wanted to do more than see him. She shouldn't, and yet...

"I'd like that," she said, and leaned over to meet his kiss halfway. Mmm... She fought the urge to catch his waist with her legs—this was her place of business, after all.

Then the telephone rang. She stiffened. Oh, no, not now. Bells on the front door jingled, and she practically whirled around to face the blond man who wandered into the shop. Suddenly everyone was an enemy.

"Is Saturday okay?" Rand asked, clearing his throat as he started putting the trash back into the

Pizza Palace sack. "That'll give me enough time to smooth out some of the—" the phone rang again, and he cocked his head at it "—rough edges," he finished in a normal voice. "You want me to get that?"

She slid off the counter to stand barefoot beside him and snatched at the phone herself, all but screeching, "No!" at him. "UnderCover, new and used books, please hold," she breathed quickly into the phone, then put down the receiver.

Rand was watching her. Was he suspicious? No, just waiting for her answer. "Saturday," she repeated, too aware of the waiting phone call to think straight. "Um…yes. Sure. Sounds wonderful."

The customer, after a moment's pause, headed toward the magic and the occult section. After the man disappeared behind the bookshelf, Rand wrapped her in his arms—and the cape—one more time. "Until then, *mademoiselle*." He ducked his head, watching her eyes all the while, then met her lips with his. Promise heated their kiss—and anticipation. *You've barely tried me.*

Then he was backing away, silk trailing off her shoulders and sweeping to the floor. He paused at the door for a low bow from the waist, then left, barely jerking the hem of his cape out of the way before the door could close on it.

There was absolutely nothing dangerous about him, she decided—then winced as she remembered the forgotten phone receiver. She didn't want to pick it up, didn't want to know.

But that was silly, completely unlike her. Against

her will, she closed her fingers around the receiver and lifted it slowly to her ear. "Don't be Jimmy," she mouthed, and asked, "Hello?"

"Hey, sis." Relief sapped her strength, and she sagged back against the counter.

"Hey, Stevie. What's up?"

"Have you read about that missing person, Tyrell Benjamin? They found him. A good piece of him, anyway. Near as the medical examiner can tell, whatever got Dennis Gareaux last month got him."

She stared unseeing at the red candle burning merrily beside her cash register. She'd chosen red today because of its romantic qualities. Now it made her think of blood. "Oh."

"Anyway, it looks like we've got a serial killer here. And I'm offering you the story."

The blond customer approached the counter with a stack of books. "Steve, I've got to put you down for a minute." She could hear the tinny noise of his protest as she placed the receiver on the shelf behind the counter and rang up the man's purchase. He'd chosen a range of New Age books—crystals, reincarnation, even psychic self-defense—and wore a tie-dyed T-shirt, and a piece of quartz on a leather thong around his neck. Maybe not a witch, but certainly her kind of customer. Normally she would ask him how he'd heard of her store's arcane selection—bookstores were quite a meeting ground in the occult community. Instead she quickly bagged his books and sent him away.

At his exit, she picked the phone back up. "Now, what were you saying?"

"I said, 'You're not putting me down again, are you?' So what about the story? You don't sound real excited."

"What about your other reporters?" He had two of them, she knew, and several free-lancers like herself.

"Nobody goes to work for the *Stagwater Sentinel* because of their great investigative drive," he said dryly. "They work here because the hours are regular and this town's a nice place to start a family. This is right along your line, sis. It's got those weirdo touches you specialize in." When she said nothing, he added, "Okay, you'd be helping yourself as much as me. Get a good story, Sylvie. Give yourself a chance to leave Stagwater."

"Why would I want to leave Stagwater?"

"You'll make a more honest decision when the opportunity arises, that's for sure. So, will you do it?"

She had no customers. She wasn't really too busy—despite the myth perpetuated by some television shows, a great deal of reporting consisted of letting your fingers do the walking. And to some extent she'd already started investigating.

"I'll give it a shot," she said with a reluctance that surprised even her, and plucked a pencil from the cup beside the register. "What have you got on this guy so far?"

"Well, if he's a true serial killer, there are already a few characteristics we can count on," said Steve.

"I know, I know. Male, Caucasian, probably in his thirties, highly intelligent." She made a few notes while she ticked off the usual points.

"Or even charismatic," Steve added—he'd once done investigative reporting himself. "I can get you a copy of the forensics report. Basically, it adds dark hair and a B negative blood type—"

"What?" Her pencil froze.

"Blood type B negative," Steve reminded her.

Give me three pints, B negative.

She didn't realize how hard she was clutching her pencil until it snapped in half.

A light mist was falling as she pulled up in front of the Deloup House, the sort of mist that blurred the windshield slightly less than using the wipers would. Combined with the spreading darkness, it isolated her, her car and the big, decrepit house from the rest of the world. She shut off the engine, cut the lights and climbed out. Moisture swallowed up the sound of her slammed door, and just walking away from the car toward the shabby porch and the front door with its rusty wolf's-head knocker was like retreating in time.

She found herself thinking of Helena, coming to visit her fiancé, only to be killed by him, and reminded herself that there was no Helena, never had been.

The door creaked open even as she mounted the porch steps, revealing a candlelit foyer. All Rand needed was a hunchbacked servant to usher her in. Instead, she got Lenny.

"Hello, S-Sylvie," he said, closing the door behind her. Trapped...but seeing a familiar face helped dispel the eeriness that had crept into her bones. "Rand said for me to ent-entertain you for a minute. You need a towel or something?"

She combed her brown bangs back from her forehead, skimming away some of the dewy mist at the same time. "No, that's fine, Len. So how have you—" The portrait that caught her attention made her forget her question, and, as if drawn, she stepped closer to it. It hadn't been there when she'd first toured Rand's house-in-progress. Now the huge giltframed portrait dominated one shabbily papered wall of the foyer. Its canvas hung in shreds, as if torn by a claw, but part of the man's face was still recognizable. She lifted a sagging piece of canvas back into place for a better look. Rand—she would know his features anywhere—but subtly different from the Rand she knew. Painted shadows lengthened his jaw, the authenticity of his pre-Civil War outfit justified his queue, and light fell across his eyes just right, bringing out their half-crazed, lupine glow. The glint of one white fang appeared at his lips, which curled in a restrained snarl. This man looked the way she imagined a werewolf would.

"That's Rodolfe," explained Lenny from behind her, and she jumped. "I painted him. Do you like it?"

She hated it. But she was saved from answering by the sound of footsteps on the now-completed stairway. Rand, looking lean and graceful in his gray blazer, descended the stairs with an auburn-haired woman, arguing about—wattage?

"You want it to be scary," the redhead insisted, waving her hands for emphasis. "Candlelight should do."

"Uh-uh, thirty watts on the attic stairs," Rand insisted. "If we have a bare bulb, it'll add a nice *Psycho* feel to the whole thing, and we won't have customers swan-diving to the second floor." He threw a brief smile toward Sylvie as they reached the foyer, a hello-I'll-be-right-with-you smile. She clung to its warmth within this cold place and tried not to superimpose the crueler image of Rodolfe over his features.

"It'll also ruin the period feel," the redhead insisted, frowning. She wore very dark lipstick—now, *she* could be a vampire—that outlined her pout quite dramatically. "If you wanted anachronisms, why not just give Rodolfe a food processor in the kitchen scene?"

"It slices, it dices, it makes honest-to-gosh Julienne fries. When you're lucky enough to have a hunk of Julienne." Rand laughed at that, so their argument couldn't be too serious. "If I wanted reality, I'd use real candles and real corpses." At that, Sylvie glanced more closely at the candle on the sconce on the wall near her. What had appeared to be a flame was actually an electric light with a flicker effect. "Okay, so we cut some corners with the corpses."

"You're impossible." The redhead sighed and turned for the first time to Sylvie. "So you made it."

Rand stepped forward with a forced chuckle, catching Sylvie around the waist and caressing her cheek with a welcoming—and welcome—kiss. Then, his teeth gritted into an obviously fake smile, he said, "Gee, leaving so soon, Terry? How time flies."

"We're going to the movies," announced Lenny happily.

"I get to choose the picture," insisted Terry, with a final wave. "Nice to meet you, Sylvie Peabody. Don't do anything I wouldn't do—wink wink, nudge nudge."

After their exit, silence immediately returned to the house. Rand's pained "Don't pay her any attention" hardly disturbed its heaviness. "She's not real polite, but she's a genius at audio-visual effects. She made these candles herself."

Good for her. "Now I don't have to feel so bad about Brie being rude."

"Was Brie rude?" Using the arm around her waist, Rand gently steered her toward the "padlocked" door to her left. "I set dinner up in the dining room. I know you said you wanted to get home early, so…" His unfinished sentence hung questioningly, and she made herself ignore it. How to explain that she still couldn't dismiss him as a suspected serial killer—and werewolf?

He'd been right in describing the dining room as elegant. It was also shadowy and dusty, but she knew enough to recognize the dust as fake, and the shadows she could live with. Dark wood paneled the walls, which matched the ten-foot-long dining room table. Two place settings were clustered at one end, china and crystal throwing back the meager light from the candelabra and the crackling fire in the fireplace. A closer look at the candles in the candelabra showed them to be the same electric design as those in the foyer, and the fire... Feeling no heat from it as she passed, and smelling no smoke, she leaned closer.

"Videotape," admitted Rand, pausing, evidently so that he wouldn't have to drop his arm from around her waist. "We've got a TV in there. Now, stop dissecting the magic." And he nudged her forward.

"You sure have covered the details," she admitted, letting him pull out a brocade-cushioned chair for her and sinking gracefully into it. The place settings were beautiful; the silverware appeared to be real silver, and antique, as well.

"Detail is my middle name. Rand Detail Garner. Did I mention what strange people my parents were?" Before sitting, he served her salad, then scooped some into the bowl in front of his own place. "We have three choices of dressing, *mademoiselle,*" he announced, again affecting an accent. "French, Italian and rancher. I mean ranch."

"Ah." She chose Italian—it tasted freshly made. While they ate their salads, she glanced across the table again. A covered silver platter dominated their half.

In horror movies something terrible always lurked on a platter like that.

"So, you've been working pretty hard?" asked Rand finally, but just a little too casually. She suddenly regretted the invisible shields she'd come to wear so naturally—and the fact that, tonight, she couldn't seem to drop them for him. Uncertainty was a vile thing.

"Not as hard as you have, I'm sure. The place looks wonderful. Well...wonderful in a spooky way."

"I don't have much time left—barely three weeks."

Barely three weeks until October, she thought with a start. Then she remembered—barely three weeks until the full moon, too.

"How old are you, Rand?" she asked, putting down her salad fork.

"Thirty," he said easily, and reached for the silver cover. She tried not to wince, half expecting a fake human head.

"Ha-*ha!*" Rand pulled off the cover with a flourish. "It's pasta! The terror of it!" She wanted to laugh with him, and at the same time part of her mourned the transience of his amusement. It could all end so soon....

Tell me where you were during the last full moon so I can stop feeling like this. But she couldn't risk the pain of him lying again. "You are a cruel man," she chided.

He grinned toothily. "I know."

So she kept her shields up, staying completely aware of and defensive against her surroundings. That meant not being sidetracked by the gleam of candlelight on soft black hair, or the sparkle of gray eyes, or the lilt of his voice. It meant not falling under his spell, even though being under his spell was part of the pleasure of his company. But could he tell the difference? Suspicion, doubt, worry...could she hide all of those behind her careful mask? But he knew what she looked like without the mask; surely he, of all people, could tell the difference.

"More wine?" he offered after clearing away the dishes, although she'd hardly touched the wine she had. He sounded stiff, almost angry.

He sounded like Rodolfe.

"No, thank you—I'm going to be driving home soon."

"How silly of me to forget." He put down the crystal decanter, with its crimson liquid. "I'd better hurry up and start the tour, or you'll miss the evening news. Let me go power up the place."

"I'm not worried about the news," she protested as he stalked out of the room. She gazed at the dark red of the wine and bit her lip in frustration. *Tell me what you were doing on the night of the last full moon.* She supposed there were ways of finding out— but only one way would do. He had to tell her. Maybe she *could* ask. Maybe he would really answer her this time.

He returned, pride and excitement lightening his momentary anger, and helped her to her feet. Maybe she could ask—but all thoughts of questioning vanished when she looked for the first time at the doorway where they'd come in.

A cold breeze of recognition chilled her at the sight

of the portrait—another portrait—that hung over that doorway.

"I, uh, was going to tell you about that," said Rand quickly, glancing at the painting and then at her again.

She continued to stare at the picture.

Unlike the painting of Rodolfe Deloup in the foyer, this portrait showed a woman. She wore a yellow gown of the same period as Rodolfe's costume, with a diamond choker around her slim neck. She had a slender, birdlike build. Her oval face showed no expression, as if she had been a lady in complete control of herself. Her large brown eyes gazed coolly out into the shadows of the dining room. And her soft brown hair feathered around her face before draping down her back.

Face-to-face with herself, Sylvie swallowed hard. "Helena?"

"When Lenny suggested—I mean, this house's Helena is different than my earlier Helena, and I wanted her portrait to show that. At my last haunted house, the legend had her become a werewolf, too. Rodolfe's mate. The townspeople shoot her, and she barely manages to drag herself home before dawn. Rodolfe vows to avenge her...." His glance flicked back to the portrait, then to her. "Anyway, I figured saying that Rodolfe killed her himself made for a better story. Which changes Helena. But we've got time to redo the picture, if it bothers you."

"Why should it bother me?" *Just because it casts me in the role of the woman whom the werewolf both loved and murdered? Don't be silly.*

The night went downhill from there.

It wasn't the fault of the house. Rand started his tour by pushing in one of the dark panels of the dining room wall—''The servant guides will know about these passages,'' he whispered—and leading her into a cramped, candlelit corridor that echoed their footsteps back at them. Their path took them around a blind corner, past which, *of course,* something would be lurking—but instead the turn led only past the back part of a two-way mirror. A faint music-box melody played somewhere nearby, repeating endlessly.

"Rodolfe has ways of spying on his guests," hissed Rand, in his role as guide. Curious, she peered closer and realized she was looking back into the shadowy dining room where they'd just eaten...but that two people were now moving in the corner of it.

Two *ghostly* people. Dancing.

One of them looked like Rand, but not the Rand who was standing beside her now. The Rand in the dining room wore a long waistcoat of crimson brocade, with a white cravat and wrist ruffles, black breeches, hose and buckled shoes. The white-and-red-gowned woman he held in his arms had long brown hair, as in the portrait, but his chest shadowed her face, and her petticoats and skirt swathed the rest of her. He clutched her against him; in fact, he carried her. She was not dancing at all. What had looked like a red design on her white gown, Sylvie realized slowly, was blood. It dripped streaks down the woman's dangling arms and stained Rand's—no, Rodolfe's—fluffy cravat. The details had eluded her at first because of the figures' transparency.

The woman was dead.

The ghostly Rand lifted his head, bared his too-sharp teeth and howled a long, lonely wolf's howl.

Slam! With a suddenness that was itself frightening, a haggard old man sprang up from beneath the other side of the mirror and launched himself against the glass. Sylvie fell back from the attack, as if he wanted to crash right through and grab her, but he only cried, "Master! Master!" and pawed at the tinted barrier.

Then the dining room fell dark.

Pressed back against the corridor's opposite wall, she made herself draw a deep breath.

"You didn't scream," Rand noted curiously. She had to look at him. Yes, his hair was still pulled back into the ponytail—which was looking more Old World the longer she knew him. But he also wore modern jeans, tank top, jacket and loafers. Here stood her Rand, not the fictitious Rodolfe...though obviously he'd somehow played the part. And he seemed honestly puzzled by her silence in the face of his house's first good scare.

"How?" she asked. Then she clarified herself. "How did you do it?"

"It didn't scare you?" The dining room candles came on again, but without the ghosts. He held up a hand and disappeared around the corner. When he came back, the music box started playing again, and the ghosts began their macabre waltz. Some sort of sensor, she realized, and even that tiny piece of reality helped balance her.

He peered into the scene, studying himself in his other incarnation. That contrast seemed more eerie than even the ghosts, though not for the reasons he'd intended.

She had only circumstantial evidence. Vague clues and silly coincidences. Lots of people had B negative blood. Lots of people were busy on the full moon. Damn it, she didn't want reality to be werewolves and ghosts anymore! "How did you do it?"

"You just aren't going to take this in the mood that it's intended, are you?" She could still see, over his shoulder, Rodolfe—him—dragging his dead lover in his insane dance. The simple tune was repeated yet again.

He shoved his hands into his jacket pockets. "Fine." But she could tell from the stubborn set of his face that it wasn't fine. "There's a pressure plate in the floor as you round the corner. That cues everything to start. In the darkest corner of the dining room I set up a big piece of plate glass at an angle, so it won't reflect any of the candlelight while you're in there. That's the surface the film of me and Terry is projected against, so it looks like the characters are in the room. And the crazed servant was Lenny, with a latex mask on." Behind him, the ghostly Rodolfe threw back his head in his despairing howl—but no servant appeared to hurl himself at the glass.

The dining room went dark.

"Lenny and Terry didn't really go to the movies

tonight—they stayed to give you a semblance of what the house is like with actors. Len's probably gone ahead to set up the next scene." Cocking his head, Rand considered her composure and said, "Maybe they shouldn't have."

"I'm sorry I don't scream when I get scared." She meant it as an apology, but it came out sounding more like a defense. Considering how his mouth tightened, she supposed he'd taken it that way. "I don't laugh very much, either. I don't cry at movies, and when I get angry I rarely shout. I'm not a real emotional person. Maybe I'm not a good tester for your haunted house."

The candles in the dining room came back on and faintly lit his hard expression. "Do you want to just go back? It'll save some of Len and Terry's night." At least he didn't say it would save his own night. Had the mood of the evening been different, perhaps this anger would not be separating them. Perhaps instead of pressing back against the wall at the appearance of the "servant," she would have ducked into Rand's arms. He could have held her, kept her safe, kissed her....

But too much had been building between them since the night of their first date, when she'd originally seen his jaunty exterior as a mask for a wilder, perhaps dangerous soul. Too many vague clues, too much silly coincidence, too few questions on her part.

"Answer one thing for me?" she asked now. One way or another, the uncertainty had to end. It wasn't much of a confrontation—but then, she wasn't confrontational by nature.

He paused, considered, and said, "Licorice."

"What?"

"You said to answer one thing.... Oh! Did you have one *specific* thing in mind?" The dimples appeared now; he was letting his anger go, trying to charm her again.

Perhaps she could have played along, but it would have been just that, mere pretense. "What were you really doing a week ago Friday?" One piece of conflicting evidence—that was all she needed.

But Rand only quirked an eyebrow at her. "I'd tell you," he said dramatically, "but then I'd have to kill you."

"Good night, Rand." She turned down the dark corridor.

"What?"

She didn't wait to see his confused—possibly hurt—expression. It would only keep her from going, and if she stayed, the wall between them would just get higher. Better to break it off now, and perhaps leave enough bits of a relationship to piece together later. If there was a later. Behind her she could hear the tinny sound of the music box beginning its plodding tune; she must have stepped on the pressure plate. She could hear Rand's footsteps, mixing with the echoes of her own. She pushed at the panel they'd come in through—and nothing happened.

His footsteps neared. She pushed the panel again, harder, trying not to become frantic. He would think she was running scared, and that wasn't it. Not exactly.

She wasn't running scared—she was just running.

The footsteps stopped right behind her. He clasped her shoulder with one hand.

She closed her eyes—then opened them when she heard a click and felt the cooler air of the dining room on her face.

"I can't." He said the words softly. His heavy hand stayed her but didn't trap her. Across the room, the ghostly Rodolfe spun with his gory partner, then howled.

The lights died—even the televised fire. She felt the weight of his hand shift, felt the warmth of his presence as he leaned nearer.

"Maybe you'd understand," he said into the darkness, his voice husky. "You're a witch. They're pretty open-minded, right?"

She turned to face him, but his fingers tightened on her shoulder and stilled her. *Now* she felt trapped. He whispered, "There's something you should know about me, and it's not an easy thing to accept. You may not want to see me after I tell you. Not that it's exactly my fault."

Suddenly she didn't want to know. *Never mind. I made a mistake. Let's start over.* "Tell me."

"The reason I stayed at the house on the night of the full moon is connected to it—sort of." His breath warmed her neck. "I couldn't leave. I—"

The electric candles came back on. Rand winced away from their slight light and flushed. "I was making sure nobody would break in,'' he said quickly, ducking his head as he stepped back. ''Can't we leave it at that?''

It was as if he'd slammed a door in her face; she could sense nothing from him at all. When she turned away, his fingers loosened enough to release her.

''I guess we have to,'' she said, defeated.

He didn't stop her from leaving.

Outside, the rain had stopped, and ground fog drifted across the lushness of the lawn, particularly in the sprawling shelter of the trees. It parted at her approach, then seeped tentatively back in her wake. The cool humidity clung moistly to her, making her hand slip on the car's door handle when she tried to open it.

''Damn!'' But it wasn't about the door. Why had she forced this?

Even once she'd strapped herself securely into the familiarity of her old Pinto, she felt the cloying dampness all around her. She started the car. Her headlights illuminated more mist, which blurred the driveway ahead of her.

Had something moved in it?

Her fingers clutched the steering wheel like talons as she leaned forward, intent on the swirl of the fog.

She'd never had a psychic vision before—but she knew one when it came to her. Gradually the mist reshaped itself, molded into near-substance, shadows that hinted at and then showed figures. A man, kneeling on the ground, sobbing over the figure in his arms.

A man with a ponytail…wearing shorts and a T-shirt. Not Rodolfe.

And limp in his embrace, staining his arms with what had to be blood, lay the object of his grief—a dead wolf.

Perhaps at a passing breeze, the mist rippled and mixed and re-formed into nothingness. The vision vanished.

Too stunned by what she'd seen—or *seen*—to react, Sylvie put her car into gear and escaped.

CHAPTER EIGHT

Dark of the Moon

Jimmy Radcliff finally called from Los Angeles. "You're not going to like this, sunshine."

Sylvie, perched behind the counter at UnderCover, was not surprised. For one thing, in the four days since Rand's near-confession, she hadn't felt much at all. Why should this be different? For another, she and Jimmy had gone through this once before.

Same girl, different boyfriend-gone-bad.

"Your Rand Garner was arrested on a murder charge not quite a year ago. The police got an anonymous tip one morning and went through some old house of his. You sure you want to hear this?"

No. "Go ahead." It came out as a croak.

"They found a mutilated corpse."

The phone receiver and the hand that held it moved away from her ear, and she shut her eyes tightly. *Don't feel it. If you don't let it in, then it's not real.* She'd avoided an embarrassing display over Eddie's criminal involvement; she could control herself over Rand's.

A voice questioned faintly from the phone on her lap. She raised the receiver to her ear in time to hear

Jimmy saying, "If you don't answer me, I'm going to hang up and call that stodgy brother of yours!"

"I'm—I'm here, Jimmy." She even opened her eyes again. Another rainy day outside.

"Did you hear what I said? They had to drop the charges. The prosecution couldn't get enough hard evidence to win over a jury. Reasonable doubt and all that."

"What kind of evidence *did* they have?" Every word wrenched her soul.

"I thought you might ask that, so I made some calls. Just a minute." She heard him flipping through papers and let her mind wander. Rand had called her on Sunday night, but she'd let her answering machine take the call. He'd reached her at the store Monday, and she'd said she couldn't talk. Avoiding him had seemed…well, if not right, necessary.

Now she knew why.

"Okay, here it is. One, no alibi. He said he was alone all night. Two, it happened in his house. And three, he had a motive. Apparently he'd threatened to kill the victim a month earlier because of some animal misdemeanor."

Despite her distress, she sat up. "Because of some what?"

"Apparently his dog got killed, and he thought the victim was responsible. The cop who took Garner's report on that one said he was really foaming at the mouth about it, like his mother had died. Think it was his familiar?"

Or his mate? Belatedly she snatched a pen from

the cup by her register and began writing on the receipt pad. "Is there any more?"

"Just that I double-checked the dates against my old lunar calendars and—coincidence of coincidences—both the dog's death and the murder victim's took place during a full moon. You sure this Garner isn't a satanist? Because if he is, I'd avoid him. Dangerous energy, those folks."

"I *am* avoiding him, Jimmy." And it makes me feel dead. She thanked her old friend and hung up the phone. Objectivity… Yeah, right. Her mind worked and reworked the news while she took more notes. They couldn't find any hard evidence? That would be stuff like fingerprints, skin and blood samples. If Rand killed as a wolf, the absence of such proof was understandable. As for his "dog"…she should have asked Jimmy what breed, but, considering the vision she'd seen in the ground fog, she suspected she already knew.

Legend said that werewolves turned back into people when they died, but legend could be wrong. Supposing that Rand were a lycanthrope—and that concept became less fantastic by the day—could he have had a mate? If he was indeed the basis for Rodolfe, was there a basis for Helena? Helena had been a werewolf herself, he'd said, until the townspeople killed her—and felt Rodolfe's vengeance.

Elbows on the counter, she braced her head in her hands and gave up on objectivity. The harder she tried to eliminate her suspicions, the stronger they grew! Now that she had this information, what was she, resident occult "expert," supposed to do with it? She couldn't imagine how she would combat the were-wolf were he a stranger to her. Would she have resorted to destroying the beast for the safety of the town? The idea seemed ludicrous now.

Equally ludicrous was the thought of doing nothing.

Bells rang and she sat up quickly, pushing her hair back off her face, then pausing in her primping when she recognized Leonard Thibodeaux's big form just inside her door. He shifted uncomfortably.

"Hello, Lenny." The calm normalcy of her own voice seemed a betrayal, somehow.

"Hello, S-Sylvie," he returned awkwardly. "Rand said for me to give you this." He stepped forward and placed a single crimson rose on her polished wooden counter. Crimson—the color of scarlet women, fiery kisses, romance novels and candles burned to draw passion.

The jar candle beside her cash register today was blue, for tranquillity. It didn't seem to be working.

"S-Sylvie?" Lenny shifted his weight, rubbing one hand up and down the side of his jeans. "Are you mad at me? For scaring you, maybe?"

"No, Lenny, of course I'm not mad." Poor guy...she wondered if he was safe, working out at the Deloup House like that. She would make sure he stayed away for the full moon, just in case.

"'Cause I'm doing something to m-make it all better."

"I'm not mad, Lenny."

He nodded jerkily. "Okay, then. I've gotta get home now." The rope of bells on the door jingled as he left.

She lifted the rose and breathed in its dusky sweetness. Rand. He'd gotten under her shields. Thoughts of him, an awareness of his existence, accompanied her everywhere, like a quiet yet worrisome companion. Though she had no idea what they could become, if anything, his continued existence was essential to her.

Even if she were the only person who suspected the truth, she could not destroy him.

Which left her only one possible—crazy—solution.

"Cure him?" repeated Brie that night, putting down her cup of coffee so fast that the dark liquid sloshed onto Sylvie's glass-topped table. "How do you plan on us doing that?"

"I don't plan on *us* doing that at all," she answered simply, warming her hands with her own mug of herbal tea. Her magpie, Hector, hopped over to investigate, and she lifted him onto her shoulder. "I plan on *me* doing that."

"And why just you?"

"Because it's become personal. We're…we're linked."

Brie winced. "You slept with him."

"No!" But the idea still appealed. Considering what she now believed he might be, she had to question her own normalcy. "You want me to try to think up paranormal explanations? Maybe we're soul mates, connected from other lives. Maybe fate brought him to my bookstore specifically because I'm the only one who can help him. Maybe—''

''Maybe you're getting a little too overconfident,'' interrupted Brie, planting her elbows on the table to lean aggressively forward. ''No offense, but I've been watching you. With all this worrying and uncertainty, you're draining your energy. And if you try to go it alone, you block your best reserve of strength—the circle. I honestly don't think you're up to trying any cures.''

''They may not require magic.'' She'd been thinking about this all afternoon. In fact, the planning had encouraged her. But Brie was right—she'd been letting confusion leech away her personal power for almost three weeks. One afternoon of renewed confidence wouldn't compensate for that. ''Let me show you some of my research. It's possible that one of these cures will actually work.''

She handed Brie her ''cures'' folder, and her sister-in-law reluctantly turned her attention to the high-lighted photocopies. A fall of fiery hair half concealed her face while she read. Except for the two women's breathing and Hector's occasional squawking comment, the duplex echoed with silence.

''Well, there you go,'' Brie said finally. ''You just have to convince him to kneel in one spot for a hundred years, call him three times by his Christian name—let's hope he's not Jewish, huh?—and all will be well.''

Sylvie frowned and snatched for the papers, but

Brie caught her wrist. Their eyes met in mutual challenge.

"Even if one of these rituals could work, how are you planning to get his cooperation?" Brie asked quietly, only then releasing her friend's wrist. "At least *think* about that."

"I suppose I'd have to tell him what I'm up to."

"And give away that you know? That would make you dangerous to him—and vice versa."

Sylvie shook her head. "I don't think—"

"And suppose none of this works unless he's already in wolf form? Any idea how you'll manage *that* confrontation in safety?"

Suddenly very tired, Sylvie dragged a hand down her face before shaking her head. "No. But we've got the same problem with Mary."

"Mary's already agreed to be locked up before the moon rises," Brie announced, collecting the cups and saucers but not standing. "Do you think Garner would be equally willing to do the bondage thing?"

"I don't know!"

"Well, you'd better find out!" Despite the force of her words, Brie left the china to take Sylvie's hands in hers, and Sylvie felt stronger for it. "Promise you won't do anything crazy without telling me," the redhead pleaded.

But Sylvie shook her head. "I can't promise you that. If I think it's the right thing to do, I'll do it. And I won't let you stop me."

"You Peabodys," said Brie, "are stubborn idiots."

Sylvie shrugged—at least stubbornness implied a certain strength. "But we're lovable. I hope."

Brie grinned. "Oh, yeah. You're lovable."

The crushed shells of the Deloup House's circular drive crunched under the Pinto's wheels as Sylvie pulled to a stop. She was early. She'd called, reached Rand's assistant, Terry, and said she would be by after work. But she'd been too tense, sitting in the near-empty bookstore, reading self-help books. She'd closed up at four.

Now she glanced at the self-help paperback that lay on her passenger seat. It claimed that alcoholics, drug addicts and even overeaters could not be cured by others—first they had to want the cure. True, the author had probably never met a werewolf—not that he knew of, anyway. But the theory did make sense, even from the Wiccan view of nonmanipulation.

She couldn't sneak around behind Rand's back looking for a cure. Much as it frightened her, she had to confront him. *There must be a solution for this; if anyone can help you, my friends and I can.* Not a great line, but the best she could think of. At worst, he would refuse her help. Even so, the circle might be able to build enough power to help him anyway, manipulation or not—even if it meant he hated her.

Okay, actually, "worst" would be him killing her to protect his grisly secret.

She ducked her head to see the Deloup House fully through her windshield. It lurked under the shelter of the oaks like a gray, earthbound hunk of the heavily clouded sky.

Just the sort of place where people would kill to protect their grisly secrets.

But not Rand. Early or not, she pulled the scarf from her hair, closed her windows and got out of the car. She'd planned to knock, but she recognized the vibrations of the porch beneath her feet as bass notes, another trial of the sound system. So she turned the antique door handle and went in by herself. Eerie music, throbbing like the soundtrack of a horror movie, swallowed her. The foyer was beginning to look familiar—not homey, of course, what with the tattered wallpaper, the looming chandelier, the brooding picture of Rodolfe Deloup and the Helena stains on the carpet, but definitely familiar.

"Hello?" she called. Futile, of course. She considered her options. She could wait here, under the piercing, lupine eyes of the portrait. She could go back outside and try to concentrate more on her book. Or she could try to find Rand.

Terry and Lenny were here, and she hadn't seen Rand in a week.

Since she knew the dining room lay to her left, she tried the door on the right. It led into a perfectly normal, if cramped, hallway. Plywood covered the floor and paneled the walls—a service corridor. When she closed the door behind her, it muffled the throbbing, eerie music. The back of the door had Foyer/Chandelier Drop written on it.

Bless his organized little heart. Now all she had to

do, judging from the vibrations still shuddering through the plywood beneath her feet, was find the sound room.

The service corridor led past several more doors with interesting notions—Library/Crazed Deloup, Chapel/Breaking Glass—before it dead-ended against a ladder. She'd worn a skirt, but it was a full prairie skirt that allowed her to move freely, as did her peasant blouse, and her boots gave her solid footing. So she climbed to the next level. Tools, read the sign on one door, and she knocked, then peeked inside, just in case, but the room stood empty. Peg-Board covered the walls, and an assortment of screwdrivers, hammers, saws, drills and staple guns hung neatly. They were labeled and in alphabetical order. With a shake of her head, she moved on. Despite the music coming through the walls around her, she began to feel very alone.

Bathroom, read one door, Submerged Corpse, another. She didn't look in any of those rooms. Submerged corpses hardly encouraged her.

"Workshop," read another door, so she cracked it and peeked in. The scent of sawdust and rubber cement assailed her, and she saw rows of heads on a series of shelves. Some were the old, dried heads of long-dead humans, faces withered, hair merely wispy clumps. Some were newer heads, still stained with blood, wearing expressions of terror. Masks, a sane part of her recognized; all the decapitated heads had white plastic necks. They were masks, stored on wig forms. She noticed some man-size costumes standing sentry beyond the shelves and stepped into the room.

A movement on the floor caught her attention first.

He was facing away from her, but she knew it was Lenny.

To her horror, his T-shirt and sandy hair were drenched with blood from the wound that gaped at his neck—she could see the torn muscles, even a bit of bone! He couldn't be alive, yet even as she watched, more blood gushed from his neck. He kicked and writhed on the floor, his artist's hands scrabbling blindly in his death throes. Lenny!

Panic tightened her throat. She wanted to fall to her knees beside him, to help him, but he had to be beyond even magical help. She wanted to run away, to pretend she knew nothing. Instead she just stood there, paralyzed.

A panel in the wall behind Lenny swung outward— a makeshift door. She shrank back, stilled herself in the shadows of the corridor like a quail trying not to be seen. Her gaze, cemented to the ground by Lenny, saw bloodstained loafers step into the room. Spattered, baggy jeans, a red-splotched towel, blood-stained hands clutching it. A lean, tanned chest beneath an open shirt, shadowed by dark hair—and, as he crouched, black hair pulled back into a ponytail.

Oh, no.

"You shouldn't have done that, Len," said Rand, balancing himself on one knee beside the carnage. Then he cocked his head, as if listening, sensing....

He began to raise his eyes.

Don't move, don't move, don't move, she commanded herself.

His eyes met hers, and widened.

She bolted. Exit—surely something said Exit! But she couldn't make herself slow down enough to read the signs she was stumbling past. When she heard Rand yell for her, she pushed through the first door she reached.

She found herself in a bedroom, dark-paneled, heavily shadowed because of the boards across the window. A huge antique bed dominated the room. In it lay a blond woman, one mutilated arm thrown across the sheets in a pool of blood. Sylvie ran through the room and out the opposite door.

Which way to safety? She squinted in the darkness as music pounded at her. She was standing in another decaying hallway, but should she go left or right? Was that Rand shouting somewhere in the labyrinth behind her? She chose left, yanked open a door and found herself face-to-face with a brick wall. She tried another, but the porcelain handle stuck. She doubled back, caught her shoulder against a wall before she recognized the corner, and groped belatedly around it and down another hall. This looked familiar— Yes, Rand had shown her this on her first tour!

Think. When she tried to concentrate, Lenny's mutilated figure loomed into her mind. *Stop. Center.*

For just a moment she managed to slow her breathing, to calm her racing nerves, to concentrate on the very air around her. She'd reached the back of the house. That meant the back stairway was nearby. Behind that curtain!

"Sylvie!"

She ducked behind the curtain and ended up beside a plain, plywood-walled stairway leading both up and down.

She fled downward, ran around a corner and almost hit another wall before she realized the route Rand had shown her the month before had been blocked off—probably when the regular stairs were completed. She spun frantically around, sure he would appear at any minute, and saw the most beautiful thing she'd ever seen.

An Exit sign.

She threw herself at the door and almost sobbed her relief when it swung open beneath her weight, and she stumbled out into the unfamiliar backyard of the Deloup House. She fled into the yard and almost immediately tripped on some vines and fell to her knees. She started to rise—and found herself face-to-face with a huge wolf.

No. It didn't make any sense. Tonight was the dark of the moon; night hadn't even fallen! She tensed, expecting the animal to attack. Instead, it watched her, head cocked. Slowly she straightened and got to her feet. Silver eyes intent, the wolf sniffed at her, its ears perked forward.

She backed away, and it plopped comfortably down on the lush, damp grass, front paws stretched in front of it, and watched her careful exit. When she bumped into something hard, she almost cried out—but it was just a wooden privacy fence, six feet high. On a normal day she wouldn't even have tried scaling it. Now she caught the splintery top without a second thought, scrabbled for purchase with her boots, and with straining arms dragged herself up until she lay across it. Boards bit into her stomach—better them than the wolf! She could hear its breath as it ran toward her. Was she imagining that? No—paws clawed at the fence beneath her own dangling boots! She rolled and dropped to safety on the other side, not caring that she landed in a graceless heap on the brown grass.

Maybe fifty feet from her, on the white curve of the drive, sat the safety of her battered yellow Pinto. She gasped in relief.

Then two bloody hands caught her shoulders, pinning her back against the fence. "What the hell are you doing?" demanded Rand. "What are you doing here?"

She shrank from his grip. In his effort to hold her, his bloody hand touched her cheek, and she began to struggle. "I won't hurt you," she heard him protesting, as if from a great distance. "Is it the blood? It's fake! What the hell is wrong?"

But now that the initial shock had ended, she struggled in earnest, kicking at him, determined to get loose. Crouching over her, he tried to keep his grip. When she managed a wild punch to his ribs, he fell back, releasing her for the split second she needed. She flew up from the ground and began running.

Her skirt twisted around her legs, trying to trip her. She could hear him behind her. Her car sat ahead—

but she didn't have her keys out! The road. She would make for the road!

A loud crack exploded from the woods, and then a sudden blow to her back sent her sprawling. She caught herself in a slide on the clamshells, at the expense of her hands, but the weight on her back forced her down flat. A warm, musky weight. Rand. She tried to get loose.

"Sylvie, wait. Wait!" His fingers dug at her shoulders; she should have listened to Brie.

Then clamshells spewed upward three feet from her head as another loud crack sounded.

A gunshot!

"Come on!" he yelled, rolling off her and pulling her up. She dived for the shelter of her car, pressing back against one of the tires and hoping she'd chosen the correct side. He stumbled past to crouch beside her, panting. Blood smeared his hands, emphasizing his menace—but he'd tackled her when he heard gunfire.

Every breath stretched into forever, more than enough time for a crazed gunman to kill them. But as one breath turned into two, then five, then ten, and no more shots sounded, she began to question her dramatic assumptions. Why would anybody shoot at either her or Rand? Especially in Stagwater!

"Here's where I try to be heroic," muttered Rand, twisting around to face the Pinto that was sheltering them, and rising, very slowly, to peek over the car's hood. Pausing, he asked, "What the hell am I looking for? A hunter with very thick glasses?"

A nervous giggle escaped her; she couldn't help herself. Of course the shots had been accidental! "A crazed gunman stalking toward us, to finish us off?"

"Not that I can see." He crouched back down beside her, feigning nonchalance. "But I'm actually pretty comfortable here for now. How about you?"

The alternative was to leave their cover. The shots probably *had* been an accident...but she nodded. "I'm fine."

Neither of them moved while they listened for gunfire and approaching footsteps. She tried to watch him from the corners of her eyes, wondering why she suddenly felt safer with him.

His bare chest rose and fell with the force of his breathing. Some of his hair had come loose in heavy, dark strands along his face. Despite his jokes, his normally dancing eyes were dead serious, and he pressed his lips tightly together. Remembering their softness, she looked quickly away.

Her scraped hands hurt, so she pressed them against her skirt. Above the oak trees that shadowed the front lawn and drive, and the thick pines that bordered the lot on either side, gray clouds thickened, mimicking the coming dusk.

"I think the shots came from the woods to the west," he noted, and she heard him shifting to take another peek. "I don't see anything now...but that's no guarantee."

Her eyes drifted toward him again; he was studying her. She met his gaze warily. The blood was fake, he'd said? What about Lenny?

She looked away with a shudder.

"Um, Syl—?" He waited for her to look back, then forged on without any acknowledgment from her. "What were you doing in the house?"

Was he trying to figure out how much she knew about Lenny's demise? She could have asked, "What were *you* doing?" But it hardly seemed wise to bring that up, trapped as she was with him. What if Lenny had known too much?

"I closed up early," she said with a shrug.

"I didn't think you scared that easily. Even when I surprised you from the hearse, you didn't actually yell or anything. But...my effect with Lenny really got to you, didn't it?"

"Your effect?" If he was referring to the torn-out throat she'd seen, he was a master of euphemism.

"Yeah, the prosthetic. It really scared you."

She actually looked at him now, closely. Her relief at even the possibility of an explanation warred against her wariness, but she nodded. It still scared her.

He lowered his eyes thoughtfully, and when he lifted them, they glowed with earnestness. "I never meant to scare you."

She arched a questioning eyebrow.

He shrugged. "Okay, yes, that's my job. But you aren't a customer, you're... The blood's mainly corn syrup and red dye, Syl. You could taste it and see— but I guess that would be pretty gross."

Very. Her stomach lurched at the thought.

"Just look at the reality of it, and it's nothing," he

assured her, shifting into a more comfortable position against the car. "See, I padded the neck to make it look thicker so I could do a scooped effect. Then I added thin layers of latex, for the torn-away skin and muscle. And I shaded the blood with blue to make the wound look even deeper."

She didn't answer.

He peeked over the Pinto's hood again and said, "It's nothing up close. As soon as we're sure our happy hunter has gone, I'll take you back into the house. Lenny and I can show you exactly how it's put together. You'll see."

Much as she wanted to believe him, it could be a ruse to get her back inside. Her eyes dropped to Rand's hands. Dyed corn syrup?

"We used a pump." He said the words a little more slowly. Was he making this up as he went along, or was he beginning to figure out just what she had thought when she came upon the scene? "Rubber bulb and tubing. Lenny squeezes it, and the blood spatters...." He hesitated. "But he got a little crazy with it...."

The heat of his gaze on her profile, and her own increasing discomfort, kept her from looking back at him. She clung to the hope that Lenny might be alive after all. Which would make her an idiot. A fair trade, for a friend's life, but no great foundation on which to build a relationship.

The crunch of clamshells announced an approaching vehicle. To her relief the car that pulled up to them was white, with the word *Sheriff* in blue on the side.

With a cautious glance toward the woods, Rand stood and offered her his bloodstained hand. After a long moment's consideration, she took it, and he pulled her to her feet. Her palm stung against his.

The dark-haired police officer in the squad car eyed them warily for a moment, speaking into his radio, then climbed quickly out. He held a first-aid box in one hand. "Holy— Who's been shot?"

What? Then Sylvie considered how the two of them must look. "Nobody," she answered quickly. "That we know of."

The officer continued to stare at them, and Rand said, "It's fake blood." He wiped his palms, then the backs of his hands, on his jeans. All he managed to do was smear the red stains.

The officer frowned. "Y'all are the folks that reported gunfire, aren't you?"

"No, that was me," announced another voice, and Terry-the-assistant strolled out of the Deloup House, a tool belt clinging to her jeans-clad hips and a tank top showing off more of her curves. "They were behind the car, so I figured it was up to me to do something." When Rand gave her a questioning look, Terry pointed at one of the few unboarded second-story windows. "I looked out from there," she explained smoothly.

"Taking cover is usually a good idea during gunfire," agreed the officer easily, making a notation in his notebook. "And you two are...?"

"This is Sylvie Peabody. She runs the bookstore off the highway," Rand said quickly, sliding a possessive arm around her. "I'm Rand Garner, and I own this house." He offered his free hand.

The officer, eyeing the stain, didn't take it.

"It's fake," Rand insisted. "This is a haunted house. A tourist attraction." The officer still stared. "For Halloween." The barest edge of annoyance was creeping into his tone; he hadn't liked the state trooper out by the east shore, either.

"Someone shot at us. Twice," Sylvie said, as much to avoid remembering his dislike of policemen as to provide information. Rand brushed her with an assessing glance. "We were…"

They were…what? She'd seen a dead body in the house and run from the man she thought was responsible? If the police took Rand in, they could match his blood to the sample they'd gotten from their murderer, and then she would have proof one way or the other. Wasn't that what she wanted?

But at what cost? As if he'd read her thoughts, he stepped back from her, his hand sliding from her waist. While the policeman waited for her to continue, Rand strolled toward the fence she'd climbed. If she wanted to escape him, now was the time.

"We were arguing," she finished smoothly. "At the first shot, Mr. Garner tackled me to the ground. After the second shot, we took cover behind the car. There weren't any shots after that, and we don't know if it was deliberate."

The policeman nodded his thanks and stepped

away to catch up with Rand and speak in hushed tones. Checking stories? In the momentary lull, Sylvie glanced at Terry. "I'm surprised you heard the shots at all," she noted. The music in the house had been very loud.

Terry rolled her almost-bare shoulders in a sleek shrug. "I know my tapes, Peabody, and those sounds weren't part of them."

"You say you were arguing. None of you fired the shots?" The officer turned to include the women in the questioning. He probably had to ask that. They shook their heads. "Hmm... Probably some poacher, gone on a drunk." He gestured toward the woods. Sylvie nodded, and when he headed that way, she and Terry followed him, tramping across browning grass and wilted autumn clover. Only when they reached the edge of the trees did she realize that Rand hadn't joined them.

The policeman peered into the shadows of the woods. "Deer season's coming up, you know." It didn't take him very long to walk the western boundary of the property, entering the trees at a few points to study the ground, scuff at something with his boot, then shake his head. He asked Sylvie if she or Rand had any reason to believe the shots were meant for them. Any threats on their lives? Any enemies? She glanced uncertainly toward where Rand was pacing a ten-foot length of the drive as if he was looking for something. How to answer that? Someone involved with the victim of that South Carolina murder could be considered an enemy.

Terry caught her eye and lifted a curious eyebrow.

"Not that I know of," Sylvie answered, as honestly as she could. With a satisfied grin, Terry waggled her fingers at them and sauntered back to the house. The redhead paused to say something to Rand, who had crouched and was poking at the packed clamshells; then she vanished inside.

Sylvie wondered where Lenny was. If the scene she'd witnessed was truly fake, why hadn't he joined in the excitement? The image of him, throat rent and blood spilt, assaulted her again. Fifteen minutes ago, she would have given years off her life for a policeman's presence.

"Then I really wouldn't worry, ma'am. There's probably no connection between you folks and those shots." At a faint squawking sound, the officer glanced up from his examination of the forest floor and strode quickly back to his squad car. She followed him. "I'll spread word to keep an eye out for poachers inside the town limits," he added, before answering his radio.

She almost felt relief as he ten-foured and pulled away. She'd actually been afraid, small town or not, that he would find some kind of proof that she or Rand were being stalked.

"Hurrah for the cavalry," muttered Rand, still investigating the shells. Crouched as he was, she couldn't see his face.

Then again, he *would* dislike the police, wouldn't he? She stepped back, wishing Lenny would show up.

"It was good of him to come so fast," she said weakly.

"I'm not arguing that...though I doubt he was real busy, considering the low— Aha!" And he plucked something from the drive.

"What is it?" She stepped closer to him as he stood, peering at the lump in his blood-grimed palm.

"A bullet. And I don't think it came from a hunting rifle. More like a .38 pistol." He blinked more closely at the bullet, then looked up at Sylvie, brows slanted in confusion and suspicion.

He said, "This thing is silver."

CHAPTER NINE

As the creaking sound of tree toads and crickets pulsed steadily from the shadows that surrounded them, Sylvie realized the sun had set. The oak tree that loomed over them, draped in Spanish moss, had become a dark creature, hulking and furry, and the dull gray of the rainy sky had blackened. Yet even in these shadows she could see a glint of light off the misshapen bullet Rand held.

His eyes also glowed in the darkness.

"A silver bullet," he repeated tightly. "Normally I would make some kind of Lone Ranger joke, but, you know, this bullet reminds me of something." He flipped the warped lump in his hand, as if trying to appear more casual than his voice indicated. "You know the connection, right? If someone was shooting silver bullets, that could mean—now don't laugh—they thought one of us was a werewolf."

She hadn't been planning to laugh. He looked too angry for laughter to exist in his presence.

"Gee, Sylvie," he continued, clipping his words, "you don't seem very surprised at that possibility." He leaned closer to her, until they were almost nose to nose, but she refused to shrink back. "You've been doing a lot of research on werewolves, haven't you? You even said there was a werewolf in Stagwater. I'd forgotten, considering how the evening continued after that, but you said those very words. A werewolf in Stagwater. Dare I ask why it was so important to know where I was during the full moon?''

She said nothing. Obviously he could make the connections by himself. What she wanted to know was how he would respond to them. Intellectually, that was all she wanted to know. Emotionally she thought she detected a shadow of hurt behind his silvery eyes and tight jaw.

''You think I'm a werewolf.''

''Not necessarily.''

He spun and stalked away a few paces, then whirled and came back. ''You think I'm some kind of animal. A killer.''

She gazed steadily at his waving hands, which were still grimed with the remnants of blood, and let him read her point in her silence.

He threw up his splayed hands. ''*It's fake!* I'm a special-effects artist. I work with blood—pretend blood. If I were a painter, would you be surprised to find paint on my hands? I'm surprised you think werewolves exist in the first place—''

''Two killings, both on consecutive full moons,'' she answered. ''Wolf fur and human hair—and saliva—found on the bodies. A wolf sighting on the last full moon. What does that indicate to *you?*''

He cocked his head; she could hardly see him now, but she could make out his silhouette. When he spoke, his voice sounded hoarse. ''That you don't trust me.''

She didn't want to hurt him…but she already had.

And he deserved to know. "You appeared in Stagwater at just the right time to be suspect, you know. Your whole house is structured around a werewolf legend, so it obviously holds some appeal for you. Did I mention that the killer is a Caucasian, probably male, with dark hair? B negative blood type, too. And you were busy on the full moon."

"The cold, hard facts, huh? With a little witch's intuition thrown in."

"No intuition," she admitted—this would have been so much easier with some. "I tried to find proof of your innocence, and I couldn't." His dark shape stood stiffly; she could feel the tension radiating from him. Well, he certainly had a right to be insulted. But he also had a right to know what she'd thought. "I still can't."

"Taste the blood," he challenged. "Come with me and we'll find Lenny." But he had to know that even Lenny being alive wouldn't be total proof.

She turned away from the darkness of him and stared down at the equally dark void at her feet. "I wish I could use my intuition, but I can't. I used to be able to feel people—did I ever tell you that? I used to be able to sense them, and I was a great judge of character, but then it stopped, and now…"

Something warm settled on her shoulder. From the protective weight of his hand, a soothing energy flowed into her, down her arm, into her chest. He wasn't evil, not now, not at this moment. But could he turn evil?

"I guess you'll have to take your chances, just like the rest of us," he said.

She turned back to him. Could she see his shape more clearly than she had a moment before? As if the faintest light was backlighting him, she could make out the line of his jaw, the plane of his shoulder, the curve of his muscled arm. Trust him? The rational Sylvie pointed out that he had not actually denied any of her "facts." He had a suspicious background. She had not seen Lenny.

He loomed closer, touched her lips with his, and the voltage that streaked through her silenced the rational Sylvie. His mouth tested hers, tasted it, sought a closer fit. His tongue flicked across her lower lip, and she let her own lips part for him. From her lash-veiled eyes, she vaguely wondered at the almost-glow now surrounding them both. She quickly dismissed it to savor his kiss, even as his lips brushed away from hers.

"Did you feel me then?" he muttered.

"Why was there a wolf in your yard?"

He groaned and took her other shoulder with his other hand, then held her firmly as his mouth covered hers again. She let her head fall back, let him taste all of her. Surely he could; she was open to him. Surely he could sense her soul through their questing, hungry kiss. She could sense his.

She could sense his soul!

"Did you—?" he gasped, drawing her to him so that he could rest his chin on her shoulder. His breath singed her ear, fluttered her hair back. She belatedly raised her hands to his bare chest, ignoring the cuts on her palms, and stroked around the leaness of his ribs to the harder planes of his back. His skin felt electric beneath her touch. "Did you feel that?"

She leaned into him, so that her thighs pressed his, so that her breasts were molded against his chest with only thin cotton to separate them, so that she could take his mouth with her own. Mmm…yes. She felt him, all right, the hunger, the frustration, the untouchable darkness of secrets, the inescapable lure of desire. And his humanity. Even if he did sometimes become a werewolf, he wasn't one now.

His cheek scratched hers. His hands splayed against her back and caressed lower, past her skirt's waistband to the curve of her rear. He pulled her even more tightly against him. Maybe if they held tightly enough, they could merge. Passion flared deep within her, deeper than it ever had—because she could sense its echo deep within him. As if with new sight, new hearing, she could sense his worry, knew he wouldn't allow that worry to stop him. And he wanted her, wanted her so badly it was an exquisite pain…but that sensation came from her, too. She tasted his mouth, his teeth, his tongue. She arched her desire against his.

He'd asked a question? She let her passion answer, for she couldn't draw breath to speak. His hands grasped handfuls of her skirt, slowly gathering the material upward so that the hem brushed the backs of her calves, her knees, her thighs. His head dropped to allow his hungry mouth to follow a curving trail down her throat, across her collarbone. A loose hank of his hair brushed her shoulder with fire.

Her fingers slid into his jeans, spreading against his hot skin until the snugness of his waistband stopped her.

His mouth skimmed over the low collar of her blouse and stroked down the slope of her breast, his breath warming the frustrating barrier of cotton. His hands slid beneath her bunched skirt to toy with her panties. Her need pulsed like an electric charge…or was that his need?

"I'm not evil," he rasped into her cleavage, while his fingers delved more intimately into the dampness of her desire. "I wouldn't hurt Lenny, I wouldn't hurt you. Please believe—"

"I believe you," she panted, then gasped her pleasure at his hands' probing. "I believe you. Oh, Rand—"

"Shh…" With a strength that surprised her, he scooped her into the darkness. One of his arms cradled her back, and his fingers pressed against the side of her breast. The other arm looped under the bareness of her knees, lifting them up against the cool dampness of his chest. Were they going toward the fence? She linked her hands behind his neck, burrowing her fingers into his hair and what remained of his ponytail. The floating sensation of being carried hardly seemed unusual after the intoxication of his lovemaking.

He nudged open some kind of latch with his hip, pushed through a gate and carried her a little farther.

How far? He'd kissed her again, partway there, and she'd lost track. Then he was lowering her feet onto a flagstone step, opening an actual door and guiding her into a dark, indoor privacy that became theirs with the click of a latch and the thud of a turned dead bolt.

The second sound echoed around them.

"It's to keep people out. I would never hurt—" He began, but she pressed up against him, and he quieted to meet her kiss. Now there was no hesitation. Her hands stroked down his hard abdomen and followed the thinning line of hair to the straining snap of his jeans. While he moaned his pleasure low in his throat, she unsnapped them, slid her fingers behind the zipper and eased it open. The back of her hand brushed his hot readiness through his briefs.

Then his hands oriented themselves on her shoulders before grazing over her collarbone, tracing and then cupping her breasts. His thumbs grazed her sensitive nipples through the fabric, and her moan matched his. His hands left her breasts, only to snatch her blouse loose from her waistband and slip beneath the cotton, deliciously rough against the softness of her skin, to reclaim their prize.

Leaning into his hands, she skimmed his jeans away from his hips. He rocked back and forth, stepping from his shoes, and when she let the denim drop he stepped out of the jeans, as well. She found the waistband of his briefs.

He lifted the filminess of her blouse over her head. Cool air touched her stomach, then her bare breasts, then the soft underskin of her arms, as the blouse wafted away into the darkness.

She molded her palm against his briefs, against his hardness. He arched back, sliding his hands around her so that her breasts met his chest. She eased his waistband down and crouched to guide the briefs down his hard thighs, knees, calves, while his hands slid past her shoulders and into her hair. As she rose, his arousal grazed her cleavage, her abdomen, the juncture of her thighs. He made short work of her skirt and panties. There. They stood in the darkness, a darkness that pulsed with the power of their desire, completely nude.

She stroked her injured palm across his jaw, past his dimple, and buried her fingers in his hair to slide out the loosened tie.

Now his kiss held no gentleness. His mouth took hers hungrily; his arms trapped her close against him.

"Bed?" she managed to gasp when he released her damp, swollen lips. A couch would suffice, a floor, a table—but they were communicating on planes far beyond the verbal. "Bed" was all she'd had the concentration to form.

"Here." A few steps, and a cool, sheeted edge touched the backs of her legs. She sank gracefully down.

"Just a sec," he muttered, and she heard him rummage in—a box? A drawer? Then she heard him tear something with his teeth. "You're sure?" he asked during this brief, lucid moment, and made a sound that might have been either chuckle or sob. "Oh, God in Heaven, please be sure!"

She reached toward him, followed along his arms to his hands, and smiled when she realized what he was doing. "Oh, yes!"

Now, when he took her in his arms, it was atop an expanse of comforter, and she stretched out on the luxury of it, momentarily letting him have his way. His roaming hands and tasting mouth, though, quickly charged her into a more active role, and she caught his face in her hands. "Now?"

"Sylvie." He petted her hair back from her face, as if he could see it. Perhaps he could. Even in the darkness she could almost see the yearning tenderness of his eyes, the softness of his mouth. Who needed light?

She slid her arms around him, hands spread to take in as much of his bare flesh as she could.

Then he was stroking her thighs farther apart, lowering himself onto her, into her, filling her.... Her breathing matched his slow strokes, then sped up as the strokes became thrusts. She lifted and locked her legs around him, riding his power. There was no wondering; she knew when he was about to peak by more than his breath, and her own body surged upward to match his. Another thrust, then another, surges of energy that threatened to, and then did, overload in an explosion of sparks, shuddering and gasps of amazement.

"Oh, Sylvie!" he panted into her bare shoulder, then managed a weak kiss before dropping his head back onto her shoulder. She felt the tender brush of his fingers against her cheek. "Now I know why they call it rapture."

Rapture. Ecstasy. Union with the divine. She turned to rest her face on his hair, glad for the weight and warmth of him on top of her. "I believe you," she whispered. "No matter what the evidence, Rand Garner, I believe you."

"I didn't know my own power," he joked, and she pushed protestingly at his bare arm. It wasn't just the sex, and he knew it.

"It's easy to think I was stupid, that I should have known your innocence, but, Rand—"

"You weren't stupid."

"It made sense."

"Shh... I know it did." He stroked her hair back from her temple, lulling her with his touch. "There are a lot of strange things in this world, Syl. You weren't stupid. But now, what makes sense—" his thumb brushed her lip "—is us."

"I still wish..."

"Stop it," he said, more firmly. "Or I'll huff, and I'll puff..."

"And you'll what?"

He blew into her hair, fluffing it back.

She giggled. "Okay, I'll be good. I promise."

"Mmm..." he purred, pushing himself up from her. "You're already good, Sylvie Peabody." And he kissed her very thoroughly.

A phone—right beside them—rang. Sylvie jumped,

then caught her breath; she hadn't realized there was a phone so close by.

"They're too late," murmured Rand against her temple, the warmth of his breath relaxing her again, even at the second ring. "Normally the phone would have rung just as we got here, but we tricked it."

"Where's here?" she thought to ask.

"My house." The phone rang again.

"I thought the Deloup House—"

"Are you crazy? You think I'd *sleep* in that place?"

There was a click, and Rand's message began. He'd changed it from the Dracula voice to a Peter Lorre imitation, announcing the dates and hours when the house would be open and listing audition times for interested actors. "This is the grandmother cottage," he whispered, then laughed, while the message continued to play. "Makes a certain sense that I'd finally get you in the grandmother's cottage."

"Hello, Rand Garner? This is Brigit Conway Peabody, and I'm looking for my sister-in-law...." Rand rolled off Sylvie to snatch the phone. She felt her way to the head of the bed, cold from his sudden absence, and slid under the covers.

"Hi, yes, she's here," he said, then paused. "Well, yes, I suppose you...could talk to her." His voice took on an eerie, sinister tone. "But I don't know if she's capable of answering you."

Sylvie reached in the direction of his voice, found the phone and pulled it away from him. "Hi, Brie, don't mind him. I'm fine." Mmm... More than fine.

"You didn't come home," Brie said accusingly. In the background, Sylvie could hear pots clanking—Steve must be doing the dishes. The image of their bright kitchen made a stark contrast to the shelter of the darkness around her. She tried to sit up, as if that would add some dignity to her situation. Rand burrowed into the covers beside her and slid one bare leg over hers. "And I thought to myself, where could Sylvie be? Surely she wouldn't do anything so stupid as to go see Rand Garner."

"I am perfectly safe, Brie." She grinned. She could sense her friend's hesitation. Brie wanted to question her, but witches didn't believe in protecting people who didn't want protection.

"Brigit," Sylvie said, more firmly. "I promise, by all the strength I call my own, in this and all worlds—*I am safe.*"

"Nice oath," Rand murmured into her ear. It tickled.

"If you let him kill you, I'll have Mary do a séance just to chew you out. I hope you know that." Brie paused, then gave in. Sylvie imagined it was a hard decision for her. "I'll want a full report."

"Tomorrow."

"Oh? With details, then."

"Gotta go." She handed the phone back to Rand and heard him settle it into its cradle. Then she settled herself onto his chest, feeling so very safe it hurt.

"I like her," he said cheerfully. "She reminds me of Terry."

At the affection in his voice, she felt herself tense.

She swallowed back the unfounded jealousy, surprised by her urge to pull him closer. Now that she'd
slept with him, she instinctively considered him hers.

Perhaps he was.

''Were does Terry stay?'' she asked casually, hoping he would assume her concern was for their own
privacy.

He did. ''Now, *she* stays in the house. It doesn't
bother her, and that way she can keep an eye on
things.'' His tone was suddenly dark, and the sudden
mood swing hit her with an almost physical force.
One moment the air around them was alight with
playfulness, the next they might have been at a fu-
neral. But why? She didn't think it was Terry....

He sat up, moved away from her and flipped on a
light by the bedside. Despite the weight of the moment, she looked around in delight. They were in a
large four-poster bed, tucked beneath a quilted blue
comforter. Dark beams contrasted with the room's
white walls. The wooden floor gleamed, and the
oaken door across the room—the one through which
they'd entered—had diamond-shaped panes of glass.
Another room lurked past the door, but it didn't look
like a large one. Of course, a grandmother's cottage
would be small.

Rand's taste seemed to lean toward heavy furniture
and bright colors—green throw pillows on a wooden
bench sofa, a bright yellow rug, a purple telephone
on his bedside table. Still, although the sheer bulk of
the furniture and the brightness of the room clamored

for her attention, the pain in his silver eyes indicated that he needed her more.

Funny, how his shaggy hair and wolfish face didn't worry her now. He wasn't dangerous. He was vulnerable.

"What is it?" she asked.

Rand looked at her. She was so graceful and composed, even when nude. God, but she was elegant! The tousled brown hair that framed her face, before swooping, longer, down her back, caught the light from his bedside lamp in ripples of gold. Concern filled her doelike eyes—concern for him.

Those invisible walls that had protected her when they'd first met were down now. Somehow he could sense that. She trusted him. And he'd gotten her into bed—stolen heaven—under false pretense.

"I should have told you something," he managed to say, despite the tightness in his throat, the pressure in his chest. What if she blamed him? What if she got up and left...okay, got up, got dressed and left? Maybe he wouldn't tell her.

But she deserved the truth.

He said, "There's something in my background, something you should know about—well, should have known about before we..." That memory calmed his fears a bit. What they had shared was more than mere sex, and she was more than an ordinary woman. As much as she trusted him, he had to trust her. "Back in South Carolina, where my first house was, I..." Come on. Trust. "I..."

"You were arrested on a murder charge," she supplied easily, extending one of her slim, graceful hands to brush a lock of hair from his face. "I know."

He blinked. He'd hoped she wouldn't be too put off by that unsavory piece of his past; his last steady date had dumped him because of it. But this was calm, even for the ever-collected Sylvie Peabody. She'd known?

He frowned, confused. Yes, he knew she was a witch, but he'd thought that was more of a New Age nature kind of thing. "How did you know?"

"I have my ways." She smiled. Watching her, especially the brown depths of her eyes, he believed she did. Then her eyes lowered in...shame? She bit her lip. "I had you checked out," she admitted.

"Checked out...how?" He was still imagining something out of a fairy tale. That was how he'd visualized her, almost from the first time he'd seen her. *Mirror, mirror, tell your tale—has Rand ever been to jail?*

"I called a friend with legal connections. He said you were charged with killing some man...."

Well, that didn't fit his imaginings at all. "You investigated me?"

Her lashes rose slightly, and when she met his eyes, she winced. Did he look as insulted as he felt? "I wanted proof of your innocence."

"No," he countered, raising a hand. "No, because even if I didn't have a record, that wouldn't make me more innocent. A record would only increase my chances of being guilty."

"You think I wanted you to be guilty?"

"I think…" Damn, what *did* he think? It hurt that she didn't trust him, that was certain. But as long as he kept secrets from her, maybe she was safer that way.

The story of his own arrest, of the murder and of his hatred still roiled thick in his soul. But he wasn't so sure of his motives for wanting to tell it anymore. Trust her?

And yet, there she sat in his bed, his comforter tucked up over her chest, her hair feathering across her slim, bare shoulders, waiting for him to reveal his secrets.

Waiting to compare notes? The woman had had him *investigated,* for crying out loud!

He slumped back against the headboard, stymied, unsure where things were supposed to go now.

"I'm sorry," she said softly.

So was he. For all he knew, she'd gotten a copy of his credit report, too. And his college transcript. And his medical records. He would have accepted a crystal ball much more easily.

Only when she moved to get out of bed did his choices solidify into sudden clarity. He snatched her wrist, stopping her, and she couldn't quite hide her nervous gasp. She turned just enough to meet his gaze, and he saw his own desperation mirrored in her depthless brown eyes.

At least she'd come. She'd known about the arrest, but still she'd come to him. Maybe there was something to be said for a relationship of mutual distrust. Especially contrasted against no relationship at all.

"The man who died," he said, after a deep breath, "was named Lucien Aleister." The name came out as a growl—even after a year, he still hated the man. His eyes focused on her pentagram, dangling enticingly against the swell of her breasts just above the edge of the comforter, and he had to swallow back his residual anger. Lucien's pentagrams had all been point down. Sylvie's was point up. Still, he gathered her against him, as much so that he wouldn't have to look at it as for the comfort of her. She fit him perfectly...or, to be fair, he fit her. "Some local cult left him in a bloody heap on the floor of my haunted house, and I was accused of killing him, because the bastard—" But he couldn't ruin the evening by telling her that.

"Shh..." From her position, curled against his chest, she watched him.

"It wasn't me who killed him," Rand said finally. "If you trust me, you'll leave it—"

Her fingers touched his lips, silencing him. She rose from his chest and replaced her hand with her lips. His relief at her acceptance made him dizzy. Desire swept through him, raising goose bumps, and he caught her up against him so that even when their mouths parted she couldn't go anywhere. He felt the stirrings of renewed passion, and considering that she was on his lap, she probably felt them, too.

Then she said, "I've made the mistake of trusting people before." She was still poised—but with a pain hidden behind those all-seeing eyes of hers. "It's hard for me."

"What, you have deep, dark secrets, too?" He'd meant it as a joke, a way to release his coiled anger at the memory of the grisly murder—and at his own, involuntary, role in it.

But she said, "Not really," a little too seriously.

"No illegitimate children? No sex-change operations? No neo-Nazi activity I should be aware of? Nothing?" Besides the witch stuff. He suspected she would resent his grouping that with the others.

"Nothing we need to go into." There it was again. Damn. He wasn't sure he could stand having her protective wall go up against him again.

But she slid up his chest, the full length of her grazing enticingly against the full length of him, until her mouth could reach his. Then she kissed him, her moist lips compelling a response, and his worries evaporated with his willpower. He buried one hand in her hair and trapped her against him by the waist with the other, then met her lips hungrily.

Okay, so he could stand it for a little while.

He seemed to feel at his sanest during the dark of the moon, when the pull of his curse reached its weakest point. But being sane wasn't helping him today.

Perhaps sanity was his downfall. He could kill— had to kill—when the madness came upon him. But in his human form?

His hand began to tremble, and he slowly withdrew the muzzle of his Saturday night special from his mouth. He let the gun clatter to the table in front of

*him. He had no more willpower, and it would only
get worse.*

Again.

*What good was it to be sane, just to recognize The
Change coming again? The dark moon was also a
new moon. In a day or so there would be a crescent
moon. Over the next two weeks it would bloom, feed-
ing on his sanity. And then he would kill again.*

Two weeks would pass too quickly.

CHAPTER TEN

Waxing Moon

She felt fully awake again.

"You're a what?" repeated Rand over breakfast in his cozy kitchen alcove. He wore only a pair of briefs and had again pulled his hair back. She wore a large purple "Haunted Deloup House" T-shirt that hung to her thighs. And they were sitting at an oak table so sturdy it would probably hold a truck as easily as the platters of pancakes Rand made.

"An empath," she repeated, wanting to share her pleasure at the return of her ability and hoping he would accept the idea.

"What am I thinking?" he asked her challengingly, and stopped spooning sugar into his second cup of coffee to squint in concentration.

Under the table, she nudged his bare leg with her bare foot, enjoying the resulting tingle of contact. She'd done a lot of tingling, both last night and this morning. "If you're pulling that routine, you obviously think I'm a telepath. Empathy isn't as complicated. It's just sensing feelings. A lot of it is a natural awareness of people's voices, eyes, posture…and maybe some more subtle, subconscious stuff like their smell or energy level. Like when a friend says hello and you know he's upset, or when someone walks by and you automatically don't trust him.''

He caught her foot between his own while he considered that. "I do that sometimes. Maybe I'm empathic, too.''

"Lots of people are. They just don't always notice it, or use it, or know what to call it.'' She trapped his foot between her own. "But some people aren't, and for a long time I haven't been.''

"Like when I get so absorbed with work that Terry has to clobber me before I realize she's in a bad mood,'' he said.

"Exactly. Except I couldn't shake it. And this morning…'' She ducked her head. "Well, since last night I feel as if I've got it back. Everything's a little brighter, a little more real.'' She took a sip of coffee and tried not to wrinkle her nose. She drank the stuff all the time when she was working at the newspaper. Since moving to Stagwater, she'd become more of an herbal-tea drinker. Maybe she would bring him a sampler box.

The realization that she was considering spending future mornings here tightened her stomach. Not that she didn't want to—she couldn't remember ever feeling this good or being so comfortable with someone. But…

"So your instincts were napping, and I woke them with a few kisses. Kind of like an erotic version of Sleeping Beauty,'' he supplied with a dimple, continuing his translation of her psychic-speak.

"Kind of,'' she concurred. A *really* erotic version. The fact that she couldn't see his shorts while they were seated gave her the illusion that he was naked, all tanned skin and lean muscles. She felt her body responding warmly. Making love with him had been...what? As exciting as the first time with a new lover could ever be, and as comfortable as if they'd been lovers for a lifetime. Or several lifetimes. It had been...

Destined?

"So how do I feel right now?" But he truly looked interested—it was a question this time, not a challenge.

That was easy, but to double-check she relaxed her mind, extending imaginary feelers. She didn't bother to analyze how much of her response she based on having seen him glance at his watch several minutes before, or the shadow of regret in his eyes, or—on the other side—the bond that linked them. Did it really matter how she knew? "I think you're feeling torn between going to work in order to get the house ready in time for October and staying here in bed with me."

His eyes widened. "Remind me never to cheat on you."

Cheat? Casual lovers couldn't cheat, only significant others, financés—and husbands. A brief moment of panic unbalanced her. She didn't want those complications, not with Rand, not yet. She didn't want to spoil anything.

"But I need to stop by the bookstore anyway," she continued, to change the topic. "In fact, I can take that bullet you found to the police. So I'd better get dressed."

"Okay—yeah." He rose from his chair and pulled hers out for her. "If you want to use the shower, it's yours," he offered, walking with her to the bedroom. He sounded suddenly uncomfortable. That made two of them. And all because of some unsubstantiated, knee-jerk reaction on her part to a casual comment on his. She didn't want them to revert to that, and she hovered in the middle of the room for a moment, wishing she were better at speaking her thoughts.

To her surprise, he put a hand to the bridge of his nose and closed his eyes in overdramatic concentration. "I feel..." he said, "I feel your dilemma. Yes, that's it, you're..." He cracked one eye to peek at her; she would have been insulted by his parody if it hadn't been so funny. "You want to throw yourself at my feet, beg me to be your love slave, but you fear rejection!"

"You think that's it, huh?" At least now she wasn't worried about hurting his feelings.

"Or, wait— No, you want to be *my* love slave. Well, why didn't you ask?"

"Rand!"

"Sylvie!" Abandoning the Madame Fortunata act for a more manly pose, he swept her into his arms, lost his balance and tumbled onto the bed with her on top of him. Her hair fell in a layered curtain around his face; his silver eyes danced up at her. "How nice of you to feel that way."

"You are crazy," she scolded down at him, but she felt warm and comfortable on his bare chest, her bare legs dangling between his, his arms secure around her. Why not go with the force of gravity? Lowering her head, she took his lower lip between hers. "Mmm..."

"Mmm-mmm." One of his hands stroked firmly

downward, past the scooped small of her back, over the curve of her rear end, and paused tantalizingly at the hem of the T-shirt. "When do you need to get to the bookstore?" he rasped.

Her breath felt shallow, shivery. "Not until ten on Saturdays."

"Do you—?"

"Yes!"

He craned his neck forward to take her mouth with his, and she let him. Her lips parted, and his tongue touched hers with the jolt of a completed electric circuit. The rise and fall of his chest beneath her quickened. She freed her arms and draped them over his shoulders, hands under his ponytail. His fingers brushed intimately beneath her T-shirt, and she moaned her pleasure.

He grinned wolfishly. "What am I feeling now?"

But she couldn't remember the words to answer.

Over an hour later, he stood outside her car to see her off. So did Rodolfe, his pet wolf. The moment she saw him, Sylvie recognized the animal that had visited the circle's binding ritual. He was magnificent, with silvery gray eyes and a thick, dark coat whose color resembled his owner's own hair.

"I hope this doesn't make me sound like a fool," said Rand. He was trying to lean his arms on her open window, but Roddy kept nudging them off with his nose. "But I'm scared to death that you'll fly away, your walls will go back up, and I'll be back where I started." He meant it; worry shadowed his eyes, and his expression was serious. Guilt at having suspected him as recently as yesterday twisted painfully in Sylvie's stomach.

"Is that any way for a wolf to talk?" she challenged, and was rewarded by the appearance of a dimple in his cheek. "For you, my shields stay down."

"I'll call you later today, just to reassure myself that you're real." He fell sideways and straightened again, pushing Roddy back. The wolf ducked his head and made a whuffing sound. His tail hit the side of the Pinto, and the noise seemed to surprise him.

"If I'm not in, I'm researching," she promised, sliding a scarf over her hair. The weather had warmed again.

"Researching what?" Ah, how quickly he'd forgotten. Maybe the rumors about men and Just One Thing were founded in truth after all.

"Researching the murders," she said gently.

"Still?"

She wrinkled her nose at him. "You were my number one suspect. Now I have to start all over."

"Well, yes, but—" He was pushed, and Roddy planted his two big forepaws, wet with dew, on her car's windowsill, wolf eyes laughing at her.

"Rand," she whispered, as she had the night of the ritual, and the wolf's erect ears flicked forward.

Rand shouldered the animal out of the way with a muttered, "Get your own girl." Then he grinned at her again, all charm. If he'd had wolf ears, they would have been perked forward, too. "Maybe this was all an elaborate ruse to throw you off my trail."

"If you were faking it last night and this morning, you must be phenomenal when you're for real."

He ducked his head. "So you're really going to try to find this guy? I didn't think you had any leads."

"No...but hopefully I'll know more by the full moon." When he leaned his head in the open window, she met his lips in a kiss that was too dear and familiar to be new.

He whispered, "Cutting it close, aren't you?"

"Wasn't it you who said never to underestimate the value of suspense?"

"I just don't like the idea...." He frowned.

"You wouldn't want me to give up my chance to stop these killings and save countless lives, would you?" Okay, so she was laying it on a little thick, but it needed saying. "Surely a modern, educated guy like you wouldn't presume upon our intimacy to interfere with my job."

"But your job is running a bookstore."

"And sometimes writing stories for the *Stagwater Sentinel.* I'm investigating the killings."

Still leaning in, he frowned, then seemed to force the frown away. "I don't want you to get hurt, that's all. Maybe you should just leave it."

"I'll be careful," she promised.

"Sure you don't need some help? Some..." Reality apparently broke that train of thought. He cut his eyes toward the looming Deloup house, which was almost pretty in the late-morning sunlight.

"You've got eleven days till October," she reminded him. "And you'd just distract me. Not trying to hide something, are you?" She'd meant it as a joke, and yet the way his gaze caught hers for a moment left the briefest impression of...what? Guilt? Even before she recognized it, it was gone, replaced with mock discomfiture. "A modern, educated guy like me? Naaah! I'm just worried you'll react to the next werewolf the same way you react to— Joke! Joke!" He caught her hands in his own, grinning again, but shadow still darkened his eyes.

"I'm a one-werewolf woman," she assured him, playing along. Another kiss finished her promise, reinforced it. Then Rand extracted himself from the open window and stepped reluctantly back from the car.

When she pulled away, she could see him in her rearview mirror, trying to watch her while he wrestled with his wolf. Despite his worry, he seemed happy.

Yet her own eyes, reflected back at her, looked hesitant. He didn't want her investigating the murders. And now that she thought about it, he hadn't answered many of last night's questions, either. He'd said that he wasn't evil, that he wouldn't hurt her, that he hadn't killed that Aleister person...but he had not at any point denied being a werewolf.

She was saved from that ridiculous train of thought by the sight of a sandy-haired man hiking down the highway toward her. He wore jeans and a purple T-shirt, much like the shirt she'd worn this morning. Lenny Thibodeaux—alive and well—waved at her. She automatically raised a weak answering hand as she drove past.

She'd nearly blown this relationship once already, through her suspicions. She wasn't about to make the same mistake again.

Despite the joy of last night, despite her relief at Lenny's well-being, Sylvie suddenly felt...empty.

* * *

The man's face, fixed in its silent scream, was a picture of agony. The fear-widened, bloodshot eyes nearly bulged from their sockets. The mouth was stretched so wide that the soft corners had split and bled a little, and more blood spilled off the protruding tongue, and from the nose, and out of the ears. And the eyes...

Rand paused, paintbrush hovering less than an inch from the lower left eyelid of the mask before him. Internal injuries might cause someone to bleed from the eyes—and, if not, it still looked terrifically gross. But the color he was using, fine for all the other gore, just didn't seem right here.

Aha! Tears, that was it. Any poor transient who'd just gotten his guts ripped out could be forgiven a few tears. That meant he had to dilute his blood mixture with some kind of clear resin.

Whistling while he worked, he dropped his brush into the turpentine jar, then covered the mason jar of blood. He didn't want any more large-scale spills like Lenny's last Friday.

He grinned. Of course, that had been the day Sylvie finally dropped the walls around her—shields, she called them—and they'd consummated their attraction. Not bad.

"I have an idea."

At Terry's voice he whirled around, knocking the mason jar over. Good thing he'd sealed it. "Hell, Terry, don't sneak up on me like that!"

His redheaded assistant stood, in her usual tank top, shorts and gimme cap, finger to cheek, ignoring his outburst. "Why don't we just turn this place into Cinderella's Castle? We can paint everything yellow and white, with gold trim, and—'' she threw her arms wide, eyes sparkling with feigned rapture ''—we could fill every available space with flowers. All those college drama students we've hired can show up in taffeta dresses and tuxedos, and we could make dance cards....''

"Gee, I dunno," he said wryly. "Taffeta is so passé. And it stains."

"Stop being so damned cheerful!" And she spun and stalked out of the workroom.

"We could put some of the corpses in taffeta!" he called after her. "I can compromise!"

"For heaven's sake, you got laid, not coronated!" she shouted back.

Rand shook his head. Good ol' Terry. She'd clearly figured out what had gone on with him and Sylvie, and if she hadn't said anything, he would have thought she wasn't happy for him.

Okay, so he'd been pretty cheerful this past week. Despite the ten- and twelve-hour days—and longer— he'd been working, he'd seen Sylvie regularly. She'd brought dinner and spent the night twice, and on Friday he'd actually gotten away at a decent enough hour to go visit *her* home. The hanging bed was particularly interesting.

She seemed a little distant occasionally—but then, she *was* the calmest damn woman he'd ever met. And she hadn't gotten any closer to finding her psycho. That could explain her distraction. He gave her Brownie points for trying.

As long as she didn't dig any further into his own secrets, he told himself firmly, he was content. Okay, so there had been a small misunderstanding about whether or not he became a bloodthirsty monster on a regular basis. When he thought about it, it had a certain mystique. Rand Garner—werewolf.

The witch and the werewolf.

Assuming one really believed in witches.

In a grove cleared of underbrush in the relatively safe woods behind Sylvie and Brie's duplex, the witches' circle gathered to observe the equinox. This time they met at sunset, as befitted an autumnal celebration. Still, the long-shadowed woods felt quiet, eerie. Night and day, light and dark, became equals...all hung suspended. But after this point on the Year Wheel, night and darkness would reign.

Sylvie shuddered at that thought.

They'd agreed to keep the rite simple. They filled a caldron—Brie's—with acorns, grains and what passed in Louisiana for autumn leaves. They spoke ancient words of thanksgiving for the year's harvest and raised a chalice of wine to the good seasons that had gone, and to those yet to come.

But with the full moon, the blood moon, barely a week away, it was difficult to remain thankful.

"'Ere is where me master—me *former* master—keeps 'is prey," said the gap-toothed, hunchbacked servant who limped through the shadows ahead of their party. He was their guide, and he claimed to have returned to the Deloup House solely to reveal the monstrosities occurring there. He was also Rand, with an incredible makeup job. The thought that her lover lurked somewhere under the patched coat, gray hair and pocked skin had a strangely arousing effect on Sylvie. First she got the hots for a bloodthirsty beast, now she felt attracted to a diseased old man. Clearly she would desire Rand in any form or frame.

The others—Cypress, Mary, Brigit and Steve, in a close clump—paid less attention to their wretched guide and more to their dank surroundings. Low moans sounded from the three thick doors ahead of them—more specifically, from the small grating in each door. "'E—me master—'ates to go 'ungry," the sexy lackey explained. "So 'e'll sometimes stock up!" His evil chuckle became a sickly cough. "Now, if I can just remember which one o' those doors is the way out... Me memory ain't so good as it was...." As his voice faded away, his eyes went vacant, and he began to pick at his filthy sleeve. It effectively distracted him, leaving his guests—*victims*—in charge of their next move.

"I'm not touching those doors, and that's a fact," stated Cypress. After the first scare, the falling chandelier, she'd loudly proclaimed her regret at coming.

"You could go back," suggested Mary softly, and a smile touched her lips. "If you want to face those zombies again." Sylvie had worried that Mary wouldn't handle the Deloup legend well, considering that tomorrow night was the full moon. But Mary seemed strong. Even her arm showed barely a mark— Mary had a way with such things.

The servant began to examine his other sleeve, oblivious to his shadowy surroundings.

Brigit gave her husband a push. "Go on, Steve. Be a man and open a door."

"How come I always have to be a man when it's something you don't want to do?" he demanded, then stepped forward. "Oh, well—a husband's work is never done. Remember that, Igor."

He threw the last comment toward their guide, who chuckled quietly to himself but otherwise ignored it. When Sylvie glared at her brother, Steve arched a questioning eyebrow back at her. Then he grasped the first rusty brass door handle.

A shriek rushed out of the darkness at him, and he backed quickly away from the door. Then he narrowed his eyes at Brie, who chortled her amusement. "Laugh it up, Red. You go next."

"But you're the—"

"And you're the feminist." While Brie stepped forward, he gave Sylvie the evil eye. "Don't think you're getting away with this, either." But she could tell he was enjoying himself. He seemed more relaxed than he'd been in a long time.

Brie hadn't even touched "Door Number Two" when something heavy thudded against the other side, snarling.

"Maybe not," she gasped, retreating to join her husband.

Okay, okay, enough delay, Sylvie thought, stepping forward and taking the final door handle. When no noise came, she pulled. Cy screamed, but Sylvie neatly sidestepped the half-mummified corpse that tumbled out.... Well, she'd known *something* would jump out at her.

"Don't try to 'ide your terror, dearie," muttered the servant, narrowing his gray eyes at her composure.

She wrinkled her nose at him, skirted Deloup's "snack" and headed for the stairs beyond it. Behind

her, Brie and Cypress commented on just how gross
the corpse was. From somewhere else in the house,
someone screamed. Sound effects, or another group
of victims being led through this chamber of horrors?

The feeling of dread she suddenly felt had little to
do with the screams or the eerie organ music playing,
albeit slightly muffled, all around them, or even the
previous scares they'd encountered. She felt dread because somewhere at the top of these stairs lay the
witches' circle. In all the excitement about the werewolf and the shooting—and now the lovemaking—
she'd forgotten to make sure Rand changed the
witches'-circle scene.

"Me master, 'e didn't take the curse well, no, 'e
didn't." The servant was resuming his narration, taking up the rear of the group as they climbed. "'E
tried everything 'e could to cure 'imself. 'Ired a
woman from deep in the swamps." At the top of the
stairs, only a curtain awaited them. She really didn't
want to go through it.

But the others were piling up behind her, not wanting to be trapped in the echoing stairwell if anything
else came after them, so she pushed through the curtain into—yes, the witches' circle.

"She was rumored to be a witch, she was," the
servant continued, while she looked mournfully
around her. Something was different.... "Me master,
'e gave 'er the choice, work 'er magic to set 'im
free—or join 'im for dinner." He sniggered evilly.
"An' 'e didn't mean as a guest!"

"I tried to tell him that my magic could not remove
the curse of his blood," said a low female voice, taking up the narrative, as a woman stepped out of the

shadows. Her hair hung, long and dark, around her shoulders, its strands mingling with the trails of dark blood that stained her white gown. Her graying skin fell away in folds from deep gashes in her cheek and neck; deathly shadows darkened her eyes. But she stood straight and tall—composed. "So I secretly began a binding spell, to contain his evil within this house. It almost worked, too…except that *you*—" she pointed at their servant guide "—gave my plans away!"

"Not me, no, not me, I'd never," the guide babbled, but their attention remained on the witch, who glided into the white-drawn circle toward the altar. Symbols still marked the circle, but not the same arcane symbols that had worried her before. These stood for zodiacal signs—perfectly harmless. The altar, too, had changed. It had no bowl for sacrificial blood, and the tools that the witch ran her hands lovingly over were not bloodstained. She stood before the altar, raised her arms and began to chant—but, though her mouth moved, no sound came out.

"That's what she was doin' when me master caught her," whispered the servant, behind them. "Just like that—though she looked a bit 'ealthier, I'd say. And then me master—"

A door across the room slammed open, and in stalked Rodolfe Deloup himself—or rather, an actor, wearing a wig that very much resembled Rand's natural hairstyle—with the wild expression of a man gone completely insane. The witch whirled to face him and gestured in a manner that made him flinch away. Then, with a snarl, he lunged at her, swinging his clawed hand at her neck, taking her down, falling on top of her behind the altar. His growls drowned her screams.

The silence that followed a moment later was worse.

Slowly Deloup straightened from behind the altar, blood dripping from his hands and mouth. Then he turned his crazed eyes on them.

"This way," suggested the guide, pointing toward a door, and the group stampeded for it. Sylvie was the last, moving more slowly, and the crazed Deloup came toward her, panting.

"This way," repeated the guide, a little more tightly.

He'd made the witch a good guy. *He'd made the witch a good guy!*

When she reached the doorway, instead of passing through it, she slid her arms around the surprised servant and kissed him. He might look like hell, but he tasted like Rand—with a touch of greasepaint. His ragged arms enfolded her; he felt strong and secure for an old hunchback.

"Grrr," said the fake Deloup, stopping beside them. Slowly she turned her attention back to him. He waved his hands at her. "I said *grrr!* Get outta here!" Planting his bloody hands on his hips, he glanced helplessly toward Rand, then back at her. "Boo?" Behind him, the witch stood up, brushing herself off.

"C'mon, milady." Rand grinned, reluctantly releasing her. His blacked-out teeth did little to detract from his charm. "There's more excitement thataway."

"Maybe there's enough excitement right here,"

she murmured into his ear, as he closed the door on the forlorn Deloup.

In the momentary privacy of the hallway, he took her mouth again. "Mmm…" He clearly agreed. "But I'm not sure the next group would understand the connection with the legend…although I can be an animal during the full moon."

Ahead of them, she heard Steve curse, and Brie and Cypress scream. Rand chuckled his best evil chuckle, grasped her hand and led her in the direction of the next scare.

The full moon.

Tomorrow.

I secretly began a binding spell, to contain his evil within this house.…

She realized that Rand was frowning speculatively at her.

When he noticed her noticing, he looked away.

CHAPTER ELEVEN

Blood Moon

By lunchtime, Sylvie knew no more than she had at the new moon. She'd blown it. The sun would set by seven. The moon would rise by eight. And someone would die.

You've done your best. Think of something else.

Instead, she called Rand.

"Arooooh! You have reached the Haunted Deloup House, Louisiana's largest haunted-house attraction, only a half-hour drive from New Orleans...." His voice continued with the location, cost and hours of operation. Finally the tone sounded.

"Hi, Rand. This is Sylvie. It's..." She checked her watch—as if she hadn't been monitoring it all morning! "It's 12:45. Give me a call when you get a chance."

She hung up and turned back to the mess before her. Instead of inventory or accounts, folders and photocopies about werewolves and serial killers covered the counter. All of them, so far, useless. Maybe her lover knew some trivia or tidbit about werewolves that she didn't.

She had to be overlooking something, some key evidence, some legendary clue.

Think of something else.

With a sigh, she reached under her counter and selected a white jar candle. White symbolized truth—and protection.

She could already feel the tug of the moon, even in broad daylight.

"Have you had lunch?" called Rand loudly. He could barely hear himself over the muffled echoes in the small closet he stood in. That he had nails in his mouth didn't help his articulation.

"I nuked a frozen dinner," called Terry. "But I ate it so fast, I can't remember what kind it was."

Hold the nail in place; find its head with the hammer. He probably shouldn't do this in near-darkness, but it would take too much time to set up and dismantle a light. He drove in the nail, then found the next loose piece of harness—the mannequin corpse of Helena, rigged to lunge out at guests, had lunged a little too vehemently. By closing time last night, she'd looked more like she was dropping from exhaustion.

"Were there any messages on the machine?" he slurred past the nails. He'd hoped Sylvie would call. She'd acted oddly last night. Oh, sure, she'd been happy about the changes he'd made to the witch room, and her friends had seemed to enjoy their VIP tour. He'd been proud of how many people had shown up for the first night, too. This should be a good season. But when he'd kissed her good-night before she got into her brother's car, she'd acted...wary. To use her own lingo, her shields had been up.

"Expecting the little missus to phone?" called Terry, too damned observant.

"Something seemed wrong last night...."

"Maybe blood and violence don't turn her on the way they do you."

He remembered the way she'd kissed him, leaving the witch room, and drove another nail. "It's probably just that murder story she's trying to break," he muttered darkly.

Outside the closet, Terry said, "Aha," in a significant tone.

Rand felt himself perk up. Maybe she could toss him some crumbs of feminine insight. "Aha, what?"

"She used to be a big-time reporter, but she left or something, huh?"

From what Sylvie had told him, the paper itself had been fairly small, a sort of avant-garde weekly. But she'd been in LA—a very big pond. Come to think of it, he didn't know why she'd left. "Or something."

"Mmm..."

He felt his mouth pulling down in a frown. "What does that mean?"

"I was just thinking what a good story it would be. For her career and all."

"Can't fault her for that." Just a few more nails and this mannequin would lunge with the best of them.

"No. But can you imagine what an even better story it would be if you turned out to be the were-wolf?"

The hammer missed, and he smashed his thumb. "Damn!" he exclaimed, nails pinging on the floor. "Son of a—" But by then he'd stuck his thumb in his mouth. He should have taken the time to set up

proper light, but hell, they were opening again in—
What time was it, twoish? About five hours.

"Problems?" called Terry through the door.

"No, nothing," Rand called back grimly. Surely
Sylvie wouldn't go out with him—make love with
him!—just to get a story. But the faintest possibility
remained, eating away at the edges of his mind. He
couldn't think of one thing, one piece of proof, to
counter Terry's scenario.

"So, were there any messages or not?" he asked,
returning to his original subject.

Terry called, "I didn't really check. I was too busy
trying to replace the missing rats. Can you believe
someone would steal fake rats? What kind of...of..."

"Rat?" he supplied.

"Very funny."

Rand turned back to his repairs. He would definitely call Sylvie.

Later.

Three-thirty-eight p.m. The unseen moon began
truly pulling at the earth. Sylvie gave the haunted
house another try.

"Hello, Haunted Deloup House!"

It took her a moment to realize she'd actually
reached a human being—a busy, tired one. "Terry?
This is Sylvie. Hi. Is Rand there?"

"Well...yes and no. You know that flat area of the
roof, with the railing?"

She knew it. "The widow's walk."

"Yeah, well, he's up there, rigging one of the mannequins to go back and forth like a sentry. He wanted

to have it done by last night, but you know how back-logged we got.''

That was three stories high! "How did he get up on the widow's walk?"

"He climbed out the attic gable. Listen, I've got to go. Some of us have work to do.''

He climbed out the gable? The image wasn't comforting. "Um, yeah. When you see him, tell him I called, okay?''

"You got it—wouldn't do to get on bad terms with the boss's lady. Gotta go now.'' She hung up without any other goodbye.

The boss's lady. Damn it, why did that make her feel so uncomfortable? It wasn't Rand—she felt more for him than she'd ever felt for any man. More, even, than she'd felt for Eddie.

Rand had climbed out onto the widow's walk?

In the quiet of the empty store, she tried something she hadn't done for a long time. She cleared her mind and tried to *sense* Rand, wherever he was.

Her instincts, which had indeed returned after her first night with Rand, had seemed to come and go over the past few weeks. She was fighting herself, wanting to feel only what she hoped for, instead of trusting what would be.

Still, she had to try…and the relief she felt was her own. He was safe.

One less thing to worry about.

The spread-out photocopies from the werewolf books taunted her. She shoved them back into their folder; she pretty much had them memorized, anyway.

There's always next month. Think about something else.

She opened a different folder, one that held clippings from the *Stagwater Sentinel*. "Local Man Killed by Dogs," read the first one. "Authorities Question Gareaux Death," read the second. Then came "New Facts Point to Murder." And after that, some of the bylines were hers. "Local Woman Attacked." "Local Man Missing." "Benjamin Declared Dead." "Police Hunt Full-Moon Killer." More recently, the frustrating "Police Claim No Leads in Full-Moon Killings."

Then, behind all those, she found "Getting Your Ghost," the first article she'd written about the house. Despite her brooding, she smiled at the picture of Rand. Another story, "Ticket to Terror," had appeared just last weekend, with a picture of the house. And she'd already submitted a third, based on her tour last night, for tomorrow's issue.

Think about something else? Okay, she really ought to make copies of the articles; newsprint only lasted so long.

Better than sitting around here!

Less than four hours to moonrise.

Barely three hours before the house opened, Rand finally got a moment with the phone. Terry had belatedly mentioned Sylvie's call. Thank God the woman worked in a haunted house; she would make a lousy receptionist.

"Thank you for calling UnderCover, new and used books. We are currently closed for the evening, but our store hours are..."

Normally he would have hung up, but what if she was screening her calls? She had been acting nervous...well, nervous for Sylvie. So he waited through the message. "Hi, beautiful." He hoped she would pick up.

She didn't.

"Sorry I didn't call you earlier. It's really a zoo around here, and when night falls, it'll only get crazier. But if you can stop by before then, I'd really love to see you for a few minutes. And I won't look like a diseased bum. Just a bum. But you're used to that." He was babbling. He cleared his throat. "Um, Syl...maybe you should just let this investigation thing rest, huh?" She probably wouldn't like that, but it was too late to take it back, even if he wanted to.

Was she there, listening to him? Surely not. Still, the idea made him nervous. "Take care."

Probably she was just being moody. That sort of thing happened around the full moon, right?

Sylvie recognized the blond teenager who bounced out of the back office at Thomas Prints. "Hi, Tiffany. How's the college fund?"

"Hi, Ms. Peabody. So far it's been my mall fund. You want that stuff copied?" Tiffany took the folder from her, then bounced back to the copier. "Ya know, Mr. Thomas really ought to get some of those self-serve copiers. Not that I'm complaining. I mean, it's interesting to look through everyone's stuff, ya know? Hey, the haunted house! Is that guy a babe, or what?"

"You've been there?" Leaning on the counter, Sylvie almost let herself be lulled into a trance by the teenager's lilting voice.

"Nah, not yet, but it's been dead in here, so I was reading Mr. Thomas's stuff on it. Sounds way cool, ya know?"

Oh, yeah—Don had printed Rand's publicity material. While the copier chugged out its copies and Tiffany switched one article for another, Sylvie studied the office supplies on sale, then the stack of desk calendars. The second of October, full moon. In barely two hours.

"Ya know, in the legend, that Deloup guy, he's a werewolf, right?" asked Tiffany now.

"Mmm…"

"So, like, is he supposed to be a voluntary or an involuntary werewolf?"

Sylvie did a double take. "Is he what?"

"Does he become a wolf whether he wants to or not, or can he change whenever he feels like it?" Tiffany gathered the copies into a separate pile and put the originals in their folder.

"I know what voluntary and involuntary—" *Hold your breath, count to three.* Something very important was happening. "How'd you get to know so much about werewolves?"

"I was reading through Mr. Thomas's stuff, like I told you. That'll be sixty-three cents. Can you handle it?"

But the information about werewolves hadn't been Rand's—it had been hers. Something important was definitely happening. "Tiffany, could I see that stuff, please? I'm really interested in werewolves myself…."

"Sure—it's back here." The teenager led the way behind the counter into Don's office.

Sylvie felt it the moment she stepped into the small, back room. Dark emotions, disturbing ones. If only she had been a telepath, maybe she could have put words or reasons to the brooding mood that clouded the office, but she couldn't. All she knew was that something was wrong with whoever spent a lot of time here. Of course, Don had lost his wife recently...but she didn't exactly sense mourning. She sensed— Damn it! Whatever it was, it wasn't good.

The place was spotless. A picture of Don and his wife, posed before a fake backdrop of autumn farmland, dominated the desk. Tiffany plopped into the office chair and pulled out the bottom drawer of the filing cabinet. "Here it is."

The sheaf of papers she laid on top of Don's own desk calendar looked just like the sheaf of papers inside Sylvie's werewolf folder.

He'd kept copies of her research!

Flipping through a few, she realized that he'd also organized them in alphabetical order by the author's last name.

"Oops!" exclaimed Tiffany, perking up at the sound of a doorbell from the outer shop. "Customer! When you're through, put it back in here—under *W* for *Werewolf.* He'd have a cow if it got misfiled. The key goes under the desk calendar." And then the teenager propelled herself from the chair and bounced out into the shop.

Sylvie sank into the chair before her legs could give way under her. There had to be connections. Think! Werewolves obviously intrigued him, yet he hadn't bothered to mention making extra copies. And he'd locked them up.

She knew Tiffany didn't have his permission to snoop through his desk; she could sense it, along with a disturbing lack of guilt on the teenager's part. Not that snooping would be such an awful idea, under the circumstances, but she was sensitive enough to feel the minor wards that anyone's private property carried and had to force herself to open the middle drawer.

Closed accounts. Organized by month and year.

She eased open the top drawer. Open accounts, alphabetical. She quickly flipped to the Haunted Deloup House account and found nothing in it but the work order for Rand's publicity material.

She frowned. There had to be something—she just knew it. Why else had she come here *this* afternoon? Why had Tiffany just been called out? *Think!*

Then she noticed the desk drawers. She tried them—locked. She she put the werewolf file away, locked the cabinet, removed the key ring and found the second key.

It opened the top desk drawer easily. She slid it open—and stared at the snub-nosed pistol lying there.

No surprise in a state with lax firearm laws, she reminded herself, but her instincts overcrowded flimsy logic.

She knew, even before she opened the box of ammunition beside it, what she would find. But she opened it anyway.

Silver-plated bullets lay atop mundane brass rounds.

She might not have found the werewolf—but she'd found the gunman.

Don had shot at her and Rand! She stared at the

weapon, which gleamed dully from its hiding place. So Don thought Rand was the werewolf?

Did he know something she didn't?

And would he try again tonight?

She glanced nervously toward the front room, glad to hear Tiffany still chattering on. Then she glanced back at the pistol. She reached for the telephone, tucked the receiver against her chin and punched in a *9,* then hesitated, finger hovering over the *1.* She'd had no right to check Don's desk; would the evidence even be admissible? Could the police get a search warrant based on her word?

Not at five o'clock on a Friday night, they sure couldn't.

The pistol waited. The few silver-plated bullets glistened, bright against their dull companions.

Instead of dialing the police, she called her own number at UnderCover on a hunch, then punched in her remote access code. The first message was from Brie, relating their plans to keep Mary at Cy's place all evening, to protect her against any possible curse. The next message was in Rand's soothing voice. *A zoo. Crazier after nightfall. Just let the investigation rest.*

When she disconnected, she felt dizzy and had to make herself breathe regularly again. Overactive imagination, right?

Outside, Tiffany was still talking. Sylvie dialed Rand's number.

"Arooooh! You have reached the Haunted Deloup House—"

She hung up.

The pistol waited. If Don came back tonight, he

might take it, might try to use it on Rand again. She wouldn't let that happen, no matter what. He didn't know Rand the way she did.

He didn't love Rand.

Sylvie had never stolen anything in her life…but she picked the silver bullets out of their box and stuffed them into her jeans pocket. Then she lifted the heavy pistol, slid it into her purse, closed the drawer and turned the key.

By six o'clock the Haunted Deloup House had become a madhouse of monsters. Several zombies, already in costume, were pacing restlessly. A mangy wolfman kept calling, "Who's got the spirit gum?" while two gargoyles tried to make their way across the break room without their wings slapping everyone else. A college-age actress in a beautiful eighteenth-century ball gown and a decaying face read a book, and one of several unappetizing servant guides rejoiced that Rand had purchased straws, so they could drink through their masks.

Rand himself hurriedly finished the last touches of makeup on a corpse, blending the gray streaks with his thumb. Normally he loved the rush of preopening excitement, the knowledge that he'd created all this. But tonight was the full moon—and he hadn't heard from Sylvie.

"Don't wipe your face or I'll have to kill you," he threatened, leaning back on his stool and turning to scan the crowd for any other emergency repairs or latecomers.

And then he saw her, just inside the doorway, looking for him. She appeared beautifully normal, in long-legged jeans and a creamy peasant blouse, with the longer portion of her downy hair tied back in a bow. Ironic, that in this melting pot of monsters the normal-looking woman was the real witch.

Then again, he had on ragged jeans, a purple De-loup House T-shirt and his headset. He also looked outwardly traditional, if scruffy.

He rose and wove his way through the crowd to meet her, wiping his hands on his jeans before gath-ering her into his arms for a long-overdue kiss. Mmm…had he been worried? Some of the cast burst into applause, and when he leaned back, Sylvie dropped her gaze shyly—or nervously? He swept a bow for both of them, then escaped with her into a quieter hallway. "You okay? I'd pretty much given up on seeing you tonight."

She adjusted the shoulder strap of her purse, and again he wondered if she was nervous about some-thing. "I closed up early today," she admitted. "I was at Don's print shop, and I found something—"

"Yo, Rand," called Terry, poking her head out the door from the break room. She wore her own headset like a choker, and her purple shirt, with the sleeves cut off, clashed with her hair. "Lenny's mom called. He's sick and can't make it tonight."

Damn. He glanced at his watch; they didn't even have an hour before opening the doors. Soon the dark-ness would be complete; the moon would rise, and people would be ready for a scare. "Who can we spare to run the ticket booth?"

His assistant nodded toward Sylvie. "Maybe the little woman can make herself useful?"

"Terry!" But even as he lunged at her, the redhead

dodged into the mob. This was all he needed! "Don't mind her," he told Sylvie, swinging the door shut again with his foot. "Abrasive is her default mode."

"Tonight's the full moon," announced Sylvie.

Damn. She was still investigating, then. If she wasn't careful, Sylvie could get herself into more danger than her "magic" could combat. He felt his chest tightening at the thought. If anything hurt her...

"What if the guy who shot at us before comes looking for werewolves?" she asked now, in that serious way of hers. He tried not to let the diminishing minutes until opening time distract him from her worry. But really! Whoever their shooter was had had lousy aim when they'd been alone in the yard in broad daylight. Rand could hardly imagine him trying again at night, with a crowd.

"He won't see any werewolves unless he pays admission, like everyone else," he joked. Thud. She was a tough audience tonight. He traced a finger up her soft jaw, flattered by her concern. "But I'll keep my eyes open, okay?" he assured her. "Listen, I'm working against a deadline here. Are you going to be all right?"

She hesitated, as if debating something, but to his vast relief, she didn't announce any plans to wander the dark swamp in search of the serial killer. Instead, she continued to watch him, perhaps to sense him, though probably all she would get was impatience and adrenaline.

Then she asked, "How hard is it to run the ticket booth?"

So here she sat, in a small, open booth by the iron gates, selling tickets to people who were willing to drive to the middle of nowhere for a good scare. While someone out there, somewhere, might be getting a far deadlier fright for free.

But Sylvie suspected that tonight she needn't worry about "out there." The moon loomed, huge and orange, past the eastern tree line. And all her instincts were screaming for her to pay attention to "in here."

She hadn't seen Rand since the house had opened.

During one lull in the traffic, she'd hurried to the house, with its flickering lights and dry-ice mist, and asked Terry where he was. "Prowling," the redhead had answered, distracted. "You didn't leave the cashbox unattended, did you?" By that time, more thrill seekers were arriving, so Sylvie had returned to her post.

Where was he?

Between ticket sales, she listened to the chirping of crickets and tree toads in the cooling night and felt useless. Rand was just busy, that was all. She couldn't realistically believe that he was the werewolf, not still, not after all they'd shared. Surely she would *sense* something if…

But that was the problem. She knew she couldn't trust her instincts in something that mattered this much. That was how she'd lost Eddie. Her fiancé had seemed like the perfect man…until he'd begun to change—staying out late, running low on money, losing weight, rarely sleeping. She hadn't wanted to notice, so her instincts had just shut down.

She should have seen it, should have intervened somehow. Instead, he'd died.

The chill and dampness of the evening drew

ghostly wisps of ground fog out of the nearby woods. The moon, in rising, had concentrated into a smaller, golden disk against the cloudless night. Werewolf or not, the killer would be stalking. And she doubted that last month's protection spell would hold through another cycle.

The snap of a twig behind her caught her attention, and she whirled around in her seat. Nothing. Isolation clung to the ticket booth like the night.

She remembered the revolver, loaded with silver bullets, in her purse. She'd taken it only to keep it out of Don Thomas's hands. But she knew how to use a pistol.

She also knew enough not to pick it up unless she was committed to using it.

She tried to swallow back her unease long enough to feel her surroundings, to reach for that "uh-oh" feeling. She realized that she was instead reaching toward her purse, and she made her hand into a fist.

What if it *was* Rand? Unbidden, the memory of identifying Eddie's body returned to her. Drug bust, they'd said, but she'd hardly listened, staring at the damage a single bullet could do.

Could she inflict that kind of destruction, even in self-defense?

What if it was *Rand?*

Suddenly she was trapped from behind by strong, male arms. Only a familiar "Boo!" countered her momentary panic. She sagged into the embrace—the *human* embrace—and closed her eyes against dizzying relief.

"You okay, beautiful?" he asked against her neck.

"Things have suddenly picked up," she murmured

languorously. When he released her so that he could circle in front of her, she couldn't hold back a laugh of joy. His grin showed his canine teeth, and the moonlight cast eerie highlights on his tanned face and dusted his dark hair. But here her lover lounged, beautifully human.

"You sound a lot happier than you did this evening," he noted, hiking himself onto the counter to check the evening's take.

"Nobody suspicious has come through," she explained, fibbing, and when he asked how she judged who was suspicious, she smiled.

"Oh. Silly me." He wrinkled his nose at her. "Relax. Nobody's going to fill me full of silver."

She watched him riffling bills, completely content...except that something was still pulling at her.

The moon.

She felt her smile falter and didn't want to think about it. Rand wasn't the werewolf. Wasn't that good enough for her?

But that meant her instincts had again been wrong. The killer *was* "out there"—while she was here, safe and completely useless. Someone else might die because she hadn't thought fast enough.

"This is great," said Rand, closing the cashbox and putting it back on the lower shelf, beside her purse. "You even put the bills in facing the same way. Want a job? Lenny can fend for himself."

Lenny...who was sick tonight! "Last month," she ventured tentatively, "when you were guarding the house, was he here?"

"Who? Lenny?" He recognized her tack and

cocked his head to consider her point. "No—but you can't think Lenny's the werewolf!"

"At one point I thought *you* were." She didn't mention how recently.

"But Lenny's so sweet, I can't even put him in any of the scenes. After what happened that time with you, he hates scaring people." Still, he didn't dismiss her idea completely. He slid off the counter to stand near her and slid his arms around her waist. "Do you sense something?"

Without some article of Lenny's, without seeing him in the flesh—or, she shuddered, the fur—she could know nothing. She'd only connected with Rand this afternoon because he was special. Maybe too special.

"No," she admitted with a sigh. "I don't feel anything either way."

Rand grinned, showing his dimples. "Let's see what we can do about that," he offered, whispering the last word against her lips and turning it into a long, soft kiss. He drew her tenderly against his T-shirted chest, and she leaned into him like a plant leaning into the sunlight that strengthened it, drinking him in. A second, deeper kiss followed. His hands skimmed down her spine, while hers slipped up to his ponytail and held his head down where she could taste him. Mmm... He shifted position, turning her against the counter. When she stepped back, her leg brushed bumpy canvas and she felt something soft and heavy land on her foot with a muffled thud.

She stopped breathing as she recognized her purse, its contents spilling out.

"Oops," murmured Rand, leaning back and glancing down.

Then he crouched and picked up the revolver.

Say something! a voice in her mind shouted. But she couldn't think of anything to say. Especially not when he expertly popped the cylinder and shook five silver bullets into his palm.

When he looked up at her, his smile had vanished. He rose again to his full height, all the while staring at her with those silver eyes, and pressed the pistol grip into her hand.

"Better keep it," he said, his voice thick and low, his gaze unwavering. He opened his hand and spilled the bullets into her open purse. "I might turn out to be the voluntary kind." And before she could think of what to do—how to explain—he'd turned and stalked away from her, into the mist, toward the house.

CHAPTER TWELVE

Full Moon

An old-fashioned clock chimed out the hours, shuddering through the house. Twelve times—midnight.

Closing time.

Around him, Rand could hear monsters and guides alike heaving sighs of relief. He knew the feeling— five hours in a heavy costume, especially for the poor actors who had to wear masks, could be sheer hell. Even with the temperature dropping into the seventies, it got pretty damn hot.

His own relief at the hour, however, had to do with dropping a different kind of mask. Since leaving six-gun Sylvie back at the ticket booth, he'd somehow managed to put on a civil face and do his job. But underneath he'd been straining at the leash. Had she really been thinking what that Saturday night special implied?

Or maybe she'd thought a different werewolf suspect would show up at the Deloup House when she'd volunteered to help out. He fingered the single silver bullet he'd slipped into his pocket. Right. The truth was that she'd been investigating him—and she'd come prepared for the worst.

He'd thought she trusted him.

"Terry, you there?" he asked now into his headset.

"More or less, boss. What can I do ya?"

"Has Sylvie left yet?"

"I sure hope not, considering that the cashbox hasn't shown up."

No, Sylvie wouldn't take off and leave the money unguarded. She might be suspicious, distant, calculating...but she was responsible. "You take charge of herding everyone home. I'm going to get her out of that booth."

"Okay, boss. But she's wearing more than a booth."

Rand took off the headset, hung it inside the door and stepped out onto the front porch. Fresh, cooling air, heavy with humidity, filled his lungs and helped revive him as ̄he trudged across the tree-shrouded lawn to the ticket booth. The moon hovered serenely toward the west. The last of the guests and the first of the actors were driving away; he waved wearily at them.

Then he saw Sylvie waiting outside the ticket booth, purse hitched over her shoulder. Moonlight caressed her serious face, paled her feathery brown hair, glowed in her eyes. She *would* look beautiful, damn it.

His anger settled into a heavier need—the need to be through all this, through the secrets, through the pretenses.

"I tallied it up," she said evenly, extending the cashbox to him. "You did pretty—" She bit off the sentence when he grasped her slender wrist before taking the metal box from her hand.

"We've got to talk," he said.

Instead of pulling free—he wasn't holding her that

tightly—she nodded. Tempting though it was to carry her to his cottage, to discuss "them" in the comfort of his den, Rand knew better. Knowing the effect she had on him, they might end up in the bedroom, with nothing resolved but sexual tension.

"I've got to do a final walk-through before locking up," he said instead, slowly opening his fingers and releasing her. "Come with me."

Again she nodded. It wasn't "Oh, darling, I'd follow you to the ends of the earth," but under the circumstances, it would do.

They left the cashbox with Terry, mounted the front porch and headed into the darkened foyer. This, he'd decided years ago, was the spookiest time of the night in a haunted house. They'd already powered down—electric bills ate him alive—so he had just a flashlight to see by.

"You came here tonight to check up on me," he stated, keeping his tone matter-of-fact.

Still, he felt a stab of disappointment when she said, "Yes." Maybe he'd hoped she would deny it.

Then she said, "I was 'checking up' to make sure you were safe."

"You weren't at all relieved to see me without extra fur or fangs?" He challenged, swinging the light over the room around them, revealing it in streaks. The darkness was broken only by the glitter of the chandelier, a sparkle of "candle" glass, a flash of Rodolfe Deloup's insane eyes and too-sharp teeth.

Sylvie pressed a little closer to him—unconsciously, he thought. "Of course I was relieved. You refused to deny my suspicions. It was nice to have them disproved by something. But that's not why I came here.'' She paused, then added, ''At least you believe that.''

''No fair mind reading,'' he protested, reluctantly putting a hand against her slim waist to guide her in the right direction. He took the same route guests followed, alert for problems. Cramped hallways became claustrophobic by flashlight. Dark scenes, coated with dust and cobwebs, sat unnaturally still and empty. Not as sure of the layout as he was, she caught hold of his belt. Her fingers tickled his hip.

''If I could read minds, this would have been a lot easier,'' she countered finally. ''All I could tell was that you were hiding something—something angry, maybe ashamed.'' Her hair brushed his bare arm as she tilted her head to look up at him. ''You still are.''

A glimpse of a corpse. A reflection of stained glass. The Helena portrait, retouched to make her blond.

''You don't have to tell me,'' she continued, her voice almost as soft as the creaks and groans of the old house. ''But I wish you would.''

He closed his eyes against the turmoil of the memories. Surely she must feel it, the piercing grief, the vicious hatred—but she didn't flinch.

So he stopped in the darkness and admitted, ''It's about the murder.''

Helena had been his darling, Rand explained. He'd always wanted a wolf, ever since his childhood, when his dad had worked in France, where so many werewolf legends had been spawned. But only when he'd returned to the States, shocking his corporate parents with his long hair and weird interests, had he adopted two cubs, all-wolf except for a slight strain of husky.

"They must have been adorable," Sylvie murmured.

"I'll show you their baby pictures sometime." He'd named them Rodolfe—Roddy, for short—and Helena, and they were beautiful. When he'd managed, by working two jobs, to earn enough money to launch his first solo haunted house, he'd named the characters of his legend after them, and they'd become the house's mascots. The first year had gor̄ ⁻eat, the second even better...until the wolves ha   ght the attention of a local cult.

"I guess they were satanists, or something like that," he said now. "I never asked too closely. Lucien Aleister was their head honcho. He wanted to borrow my wolves for some kind of ceremony—said because wolves had this evil reputation, their worship would benefit him. And I said no." And that was when the trouble had started. A note, written in blood. People in town—dressed all in black—watching him. A dead chicken on his front step, and him a vegetarian! Aleister had shown up on the morning of the full moon to demand the use of a wolf again. *Do you see now that you cannot fight our forces?* the man had asked. *Not really,* Rand had answered tightly. *I see an overweight idiot with a Hitler moustache and delusions of godhood. Excuse me—demonhood. And if your little club doesn't stop harrassing me, I'm calling the police.*

Aleister had turned bright red and responded with the classic villain's line—*You'll regret this!*—and Rand had laughed at him. That night the alarm system had woken him. He'd left the van he'd been sleeping in, flashlight and rifle in hand, and gone to investigate—and found her. His wolf. Dead.

"They'd…um…" he tried to describe it, so Sylvie could understand what had happened next, why he'd become so insanely angry. But when he tried to form the words, his throat closed, and he had to swallow hard to regain his voice. He'd raised her from a cub; she and Roddy had been his constant companions. And those bastards had tortured and killed her. It had taken him almost an hour to collect himself, to call the police—for all the good it did. "I'd disturbed the evidence." He didn't mention that he'd disturbed it by gathering Helena's lifeless form against him and rocking her, crying, listening to Roddy's anguished howl echoing outside. "They couldn't find any fingerprints. And it wasn't much of a crime, from the police department's point of view. Property damage. Can you believe it? A living, breathing creature, only three years old, is tortured to death, and they're telling me I could try to sue for damages, but wolf mongrels can't cost that much. I've never felt so—"

Murderous.

Sylvie stayed where she was, warm beside him, arm around his waist. Thank God she hadn't run screaming from him.

Yet.

"So I…um…" This was the tricky part. "I threatened to kill Lucien Aleister—in front of witnesses. I tracked him down in his supermarket—yeah, I know, I used to call it Sack-and-Satan—and I shoved him into a rack of soup cans and said he had one week to turn himself and his buddies in, or I was going to make him pay even if I had to kill him. And I meant it, Syl. I swear I meant it. You need to know that about me.'' He dared to shine the flashlight close enough to meet her eyes, and they held no rebuke.

All she said was "Go on."

Instead of turning himself in, Aleister had gotten a restraining order. Rand had hired a private investigator to expose the cult and found a lawyer to tack animal cruelty charges onto the property damage. He'd known something had gone wrong with his plan, though, when the alarms went off again on the night of the next full moon. This time, he hadn't been so stupid as to go into the house alone—Roddy was safe, having slept with him, and he wasn't about to disturb more evidence. Only once the police arrived had he entered the house, wondering what poor animal he would find this time.

The "poor animal" had been Lucien Aleister. He'd died in much the same way Helena had, tortured and mutilated. And the murder weapon had lain beside him—a meat cleaver Rand had used as a prop in the house. "So they arrested me."

He decided not to relate the nightmare of jail and the legal system; he felt uncomfortably powerless just thinking about it. Only the skill of his lawyer—pointing out that Aleister hadn't been killed on the premises, and that there were no prints on the cleaver—had saved Rand from an even more horrifying ordeal than the arraignment.

"And what's scary," he admitted now, "is that I don't even feel worry for the guy. I kept thinking, even if I go to prison, at least the bastard's dead. At least he suffered."

"Who do you think killed him?" asked Sylvie, still

not pulling away. Against his better judgment, he felt the tightness within him relax. She knew the demons he carried now, and she wasn't running.

"The investigator I hired thought other members of the cult resented the attention I'd focused on them and blamed Aleister. So they killed two birds with one stone—so to speak. By then I just wanted an end to it. I sold the house, packed up my things and started searching for another location. I got a letter from the investigator a few months back saying that some more cult leaders died when their car got hit by a train. Ironic, huh?"

"Karma," she agreed. Around them, the darkness pressed in, and the house was incredibly silent—the actors must have left long ago, and even Terry had probably gone out for a drink.

Sylvie didn't say anything else, but he wished she would. He had to know, once and for all, where he stood with her. Maybe she just needed time.

Or maybe her silence was her answer.

He started walking again, leading her up a flight of stairs and through the curtain at the top. When he flashed the light downward, it revealed the zodiacal signs on the witches' circle. Sylvie remained silent—a bad sign, he thought.

"I've got to check the room off this one, and it's pretty cramped," he said. "Why don't you wait here?" If she wanted to leave, that would give her the perfect chance.

She released his belt. The warmth of her dropped away from him, and he ducked into a side room where the witch and Rodolfe number three stayed "backstage" between appearances. He felt odd without her under his arm.

Why wouldn't she say anything? Was there anything left to say? On the same night he'd proved he wasn't an outward monster, he'd shown her the inner one. Maybe right now she was slipping down the stairs, toward safety.

He slashed his light around the room. Folding chairs. A soft-drink can—empty. A dirty towel.

Eyes.

How could she assure him that he didn't frighten her anymore?

Sylvie waited where he'd left her and watched the glow of his light disappear into the room beyond. She heard a floorboard creak. Then she heard a thud, and the light changed suddenly, as if he'd dropped the flashlight.

"Don't hurt yourself," she called.

He didn't answer.

A sudden dread struck her, stealing her breath and unbalancing her. *Center,* she told herself. *Ground. Reach for him.*

She took three deep breaths to put herself in the right mind-set. Then she tried to picture him, expanding her mind toward him, just as she had this afternoon.

She felt nothing. Don? She hadn't heard a gunshot—but Don's gun was somewhere at the bottom of her purse, amid spare change and silver bullets. Suppose he had a silver knife, or a club?

"Rand!" she called, on the chance that her instincts were wrong, on the chance that he really was just trying to scare her. But even as she called she groped through the darkness toward the faintly glowing doorway. She should get help, but she couldn't waste the time. Maybe he'd just fallen and hit his head. Maybe...

In her hurry, she hit her shoulder painfully on the doorjamb as she entered the room. The flashlight lay on the floor, its beam reflecting off one of the walls, giving enough light for her to see Rand lying beside it. She couldn't clearly see the stripes that tore his jaw and neck, but she knew the smell of blood.

Behind him, face in shadow, crouched the werewolf.

At the sight of Rand sprawled there—*dead?*—a numbing calm descended on her.

The creature stood on two feet, like a man, but she could make out the silhouette of upright ears, gleaming dead eyes, white fangs. Fur blanketed its shoulders. In the dark silence, it growled at her.

And Rand stirred.

Galvanized into action, beyond all coherent thought in her relief that Rand was alive, she stepped fully into the room and grasped what looked like an aluminum folding chair.

She swung.

The shock of the impact hurt her arms, but the beast yelped and crouched back, away from Rand. And turned its malevolent attention to her.

She swung the chair again, her arms already aching from the struggle. The werewolf, rearing back, snarled, and she could feel its rage and frustration buffeting her in evil waves.

At her feet, Rand groaned and tried to push himself

up. The monster's attention dropped to him. She swung again, to recapture it.

Stay down, she thought desperately to Rand.

He slumped back to the floor.

"Want to get me?" she whispered, poking her bulky weapon forward again, like a lion tamer. The chair sagged as her trembling arms weakened; she hauled it back up. "Want to get me? Come on, puppy, puppy, puppy! Come and get me, then."

Never corner a wild animal. Never tease a dog. Never— But she would break whatever rules it took to get this creature away from Rand.

"Come on," she said, practically snarling herself. And then she threw the chair at it, turned and ran out the door and into the darkness.

Please, follow me, she prayed. *I'm fresh blood.* She heard running footsteps echoing her own, heard heavy panting. It *was* following her! She hadn't planned past that; she didn't know the house well enough to lead it out or trick it. Her only weapon wasn't loaded and she didn't have time to dig for it, yet she had to find *something.*

The candle trees! As she ran toward the spot where she remembered seeing one, the panting grew louder. Suddenly hands—claws?—gripped her shoulders, digging into them as she fell forward under the werewolf's surprising strength. Fetid breath dampened her cheek. She tried to roll away, and the creature's teeth sank into her shoulder instead of her neck. She cried out at the pain, struggled, but it was so strong! She kicked out. It reared back off her with a snarl. She rolled to face it, and one arm tangled in her purse's shoulder strap. If only she could see! She swung a fist in the direction of its head and hit what felt like its muzzle. Its breath, the stench of death, heated her face again. She cringed back, and her elbow touched something cold, rough. Without thinking, she clamped her fingers around it—it was the base of the candle tree!—and yanked it down atop them both with a crack. Fake candles snapped; their glass bulbs shattered. The wolf yelped again, more in surprise than pain, and crouched back, moving off her. It halted, growling deep in the darkness.

Trying to sense its location, she slid her legs beneath her, ignoring the bite of glass shards through her jeans, and got a better grip on the candle tree. She tried to hold it between her and the werewolf, like a quarterstaff. Her shoulder throbbed; the purse, which had slid down her arm, hampered her agility. The candle tree weighed far more than the chair. Could she raise it high enough to defend herself?

Somewhere in the shadows the monster snarled again, circling her. The growl seemed to get louder— Where was it? Which way was it coming from?

She twisted in one direction, then another. The werewolf seemed behind her, either way. Okay, then, sense it! Deep breath, deep breath. She cleared her mind, reached, touched...guilt. Grief. Rage—almost on top of her!

Suddenly a streak of light cut the darkness like a blade, zigged past her and struck the werewolf in the face, frighteningly close. She rolled out of its way, losing the candle tree in her escape. Captured in the beam, the beast ducked its head—somehow its shiny, dead eyes still faced into the light—and fell back.

The beam darted wild again. Rand's flashlight clattered to the floor, providing only scant illumination, and Rand himself stalked into the room, dragging a chair behind him. Dark, shiny blood coated the left side of his neck and had spilled onto his T-shirt. His shaggy hair, fallen loose, stuck in strands against the wound. But his eyes burned with fury.

"Get away from it, Syl," he growled.

She slid farther back, away from the werewolf, toward the altar.

He strode closer, circling the beast, which straightened to its two-footed stance, then charged. He swung the chair. The werewolf caught it, though with a yelp of pain, and yanked it free.

The chair clattered to the floor.

Sylvie bolted from the altar. She could vaguely make out the shape of the witchly props—the chalice, the candlestick...the athame? But athames were never used to cut anything, *ever*. The candlestick, then...

No. The gun.

She dug into her purse, ignoring the throbbing of her shoulder as she yanked the heavy .38 from its depths, then found a few of the silver bullets. One clattered to the altar in her hurry—vaguely sacrilegious, that—while she fumbled to release the revolver's cylinder. She fed three bullets into its chambers, trying to harden herself against what she meant to do. "Harm none" did *not* include self-defense.

Unarmed, Rand charged the werewolf. Both of them went down in a snarling mass. As Rand lunged for the candle tree, the werewolf rolled on top of him in a blur of gray fur, snapping at him, pummeling him and hitting his open wound. Rand screamed an obscenity and momentarily kicked the creature off him, then grasped the candle tree and, kneeling, swung. The beast crouched back, snarling, its clawed hands knotted in rage.

Sylvie raised the pistol, pulled back the hammer— and stared.

The beast had hands? The flashlight lay across the room, shining more toward her than Rand and the werewolf. But if she squinted against its direct light, she could almost make out a second set of eyes, in the shadows of the beast's throat. These eyes weren't dead.

Her shields faltered.

Loss. Insanity. Pain. She clutched at the altar lest she fall back from the vortex of violent emotion, and the revolver swayed. Overwhelming, too-familiar grief...

Rand sprang to his feet, staggered, tried to swing the candle tree one-handed. The werewolf dodged easily as the iron stand grazed its—ankles?

She laid the revolver on the altar, within reach, and raised the black-handled athame instead. She'd been right in supposing it was a true witch's tool—power thrilled through it at her touch, its energy almost visible in the shadowy room.

The werewolf's eyes, both sets, darted toward her.

"Oh, no, you don't," snarled Rand, stepping between them and swinging again with a force that caused him to cry out—but the candle tree struck the distracted creature in the side. It doubled over, stumbled back, but readied itself for another attack.

Sylvie gathered her strength and her nerves and tried to ignore her throbbing shoulder. Three deep breaths. *Stand up straight,* her father had always told her, never realizing the aural flare good posture and secure footing produced.

Rand, also hunched over, faced the wolf, panting. Blood stained his shoulder and chest. He waited, teeth bared, meeting the creature's glare with his own.

The wolf edged to one side, trying to go around him, darting nervous glances toward her. It could feel the building power. Rand moved to stay between them, dragging the candle tree.

She'd never tried to harness so much power by herself, without Brie's strength or Cy's anchor. But she refused to let insecurity weaken the roiling energy that was spiraling faster and faster about her. They were natural powers, after all: the powers of dark and light; the powers of the sun, moon and stars; the powers of earth, air, fire and water. She had only to direct them. She raised her athame, the gleaming apex of the cone of energy, and said simply, "Stop!"

Whether it sensed the power she was directing toward it, or whether it responded only to her tone, the werewolf wheeled its head in her direction.

Belief meant nothing—only knowledge would sway the forces of nature that whirled, unseen, about them. "Stop," she repeated, voice clear, despite the task of controlling the building spiral. Not yet. She would sense when. "And be cured!"

She tried not to notice Rand taking a step back from the beast, tried not to notice anything except the spell she was drawing this creature into. "As it is told from olden times, so shall I now release you."

It—he—gazed at her, both the fake dead eyes of the wolf's head and the living eyes in the shadows below those, desperate. She'd once known the same grief, the same loss. She drew a deep breath, praying that she was right.

"Donovan Allen Thomas!"

The creature fell back, as if struck. Then it snarled.

Her arms trembled from the force of holding the athame steady against the power that surged through her and into her words. "Donovan Allen Thomas!"

It doubled over, staggered—and she pointed the knife directly at it.

"Donovan Allen Thomas! Thrice I address you by your Christian name, for you are man!" Energy shuddered through her, the whole roiling spiral of it using her as its conduit before shooting toward the creature. A roaring in her ears, a dizziness, a blinding yellow light—she swayed, fought to retain control long enough to bind the spell. "This is my will!"

Her own voice echoed back at her in the sudden, thick silence as all the power left her to find its mark.

She whispered, "So must it be."

CHAPTER THIRTEEN

Moonset

Slowly she lowered the athame. Her legs began to tremble and she supported herself against the fake altar long enough to stagger around it, then sank to the floor, staring.

The werewolf crumpled into a huddle, whimpering. The whimpers grew louder, then broke and began to sound like sobs. Then the beast was crying, except that its fur was melting back—no, the wolfskin Don had been wearing was sliding down, off his shoulders. The head thudded hollowly onto the floor, lips curled in an immortal snarl, fake eyes staring at nothing.

Rand leaned tiredly against the wall, chest rising and falling with his breath, candle tree still hanging from his good hand. He stared at Don, then at Sylvie, then at Don. "Damn," he whispered.

"Get the skin away from him," she suggested softly.

"I'd rather bash his brains in—but I don't think I have the strength." He approached the printer cautiously, but the balding man was still curled into the fetal position, sobbing, rocking. Don didn't notice him snag the fur gingerly by one ear and drag it away from him.

He pulled the matted skin over to Sylvie and half

fell to sit beside her. He stared at her in the faint reflection of the flashlight, his silver eyes probing, searching. *I'm okay,* she thought at him. Did he hear her?

With a heartfelt moan, he sagged toward her, leaned his sweaty forehead against hers and met her lips in a tired, gloriously alive and human kiss. He smelled like blood—his own blood, his life force. She didn't mind. Then he murmured against her lips, "Take the flashlight and go call the police."

"Would you need the flashlight to do it?" she whispered back.

"I know this place like the back of my hand, but you shouldn't stay with this...with him."

"I'm the one who cured him." Matching his scowl, she added, for his benefit, "Or, in any case, the one he *believes* cured him. I can control him better than you. And you know how to turn all these lights back on."

He was no longer leaning against her. "I don't want to leave you alone with him!"

"And I refuse to leave *you* alone with him. Besides, I have the gun."

"You've got the gun?" he repeated, staring.

She nodded.

"Why the hell didn't you use it?"

She met his questioning eyes evenly, reading his confusion clearly enough to know he wouldn't fully understand—not unless he ever became an empath. *Because I didn't want to feel him die.* "If the spell hadn't worked," she said, honestly, "I would have."

He reconsidered that, sighed and rolled tiredly to his feet. He stalked to the door before pausing to turn and point at her. "Okay, I'll go. But *you* have to go next time!"

Did she see the shadow of a dimple as he turned away?

"I promise," she whispered softly to the empty doorway. Other promises would have to wait until later.

The lights flooded on, the police and the paramedics came, and the midnight horror slowly dissolved into early-morning bureaucracy. The handcuffs seemed to rouse Don from his misery; he glanced up, confused, blood smeared across his mouth.

Her blood, or Rand's? Sylvie pressed a hand to her mouth.

"He's not a wolf tonight?" asked Don, staring at Rand. He began to twist in the policemen's grip. "But he's a wolf, too!"

"I cured him," Sylvie assured him quickly, and he quieted.

"Good," he muttered. "Oh, good. I'm glad I missed, then."

"Thanks," mouthed one of the officers softly.

"So, since he read the same information you had, he believed in that cure?" Rand asked as they left a few minutes later. Paramedics had cleaned and bandaged his neck and Sylvie's shoulder, administering pain medication and advising them to see their doctors in the morning.

"It worked, didn't it?" she said, glad for his steadying hand on her elbow as they descended the stairs. "For whatever reason, it worked. Spells harness natural energies, remember. I'm just glad I knew his middle name.''

They stepped out onto the front porch in time to see the police load Don into the back of a sheriff's car. When the white-and-blue vehicles pulled away, only Sylvie, Rand and the moon were left.

Crickets, toads and frogs croaked from the wooded darkness that encircled the yard. A definite chill dampened the humid air—maybe autumn really was here. When Rand sat on the porch, Sylvie sank down beside him and curled into his uninjured side, glad for the protection of his arm around her. Their combined energy blanketed them. The moon, huge and low on the western horizon, had turned a harvest gold, framed between silhouetted trees and black heaven.

Rand couldn't help teasing her. ''So there wasn't a werewolf after all.''

''Oh, Don's a lycanthrope, all right,'' she countered. ''Clinically, I'd bet, though we'll have to wait for the reports from Mandeville to be sure. You think the fact that he disguised himself instead of shape-shifting makes him less a werewolf?'' She'd hardly had to extend her instincts toward the printer to trace the source of his madness. Plugging into the legend through Rand's fliers, Don must have given himself a false sense of control over his wife's death by imagining responsibility. So he'd clung to the delusion…in much the same way she'd assumed guilt for Eddie's death. If she could have stopped tragedy once, she could stop it again, right?

She squirmed slightly against Rand's side to better see his moonlit profile, then smiled and laid her cheek on his shoulder. Wrong. She didn't need to worry about control—he could take care of himself, and her, too…if she ever needed it.

Somewhere, deep inside her, some piece of glacial wall cracked and fell away.

"You know," Rand pointed out, "if we were both bitten by a lycanthrope, there are consequences. Now we're going to turn into wolves, too, every full moon. But voluntarily. Instead of putting on a wolfskin, all we need to do is strip down to our howls." He leaned back a bit; lying against him, she reclined, too.

"I'm not overly worried about the beast in you," she assured him, propping herself more securely against his chest. "Though your teeth are pretty impressive."

"The better to…well…" He grinned, showing them off. "There's an old French proverb you ought to know. *'Pour ranger le loup, il faut le marier.'* It means 'To tame a wolf, one has to marry him.'"

The barest of breezes touched her cheek, lulling her. Was he saying what she hoped—? He was watching her intently.

"You made that up," she said softly.

"Did not. Ask any old Frenchman!" He narrowed his silver eyes, his lips parted slightly. He was the most attractive man she'd ever known—inside and out. She met his lips in a soft, feathery kiss, and he captured her with a jeaned leg. "I couldn't stand to lose you, Syl," he added, more sincerely. "Not tonight, not ever. I—"

The end of his sentence was lost against her mouth. His lips parted hers; his tongue explored the hot moisture of her mouth, while his hands roamed across her thighs.

When they parted for breath, she said, "I love you, too. Yes."

"How'd you know I was going to say— Oh." His hand massaged her hip and traced the outline of her panties beneath her jeans. She stretched to kiss him again, and he protested. "Wait. While I can still talk."

She blinked at him as the roiling current between them paused in its heated buildup, a wave about to crash.

"Are you going to keep *feeling* me like that?" He asked it so plaintively that she laughed out loud—she supposed she would probably be laughing a lot from now on. And she nodded, tickling him with her hair.

"Good," he growled, drawing her more tightly to him.

And it felt terrific.

* * * * *

Silhouette Romance introduces tales of
enchanted love and things beyond explanation
in the new series

Soulmates

Couples destined for each other are brought
together by the powerful magic of love....

A precious gift brings
A HUSBAND IN HER EYES
by Karen Rose Smith (on sale March 2002)

Dreams come true in
CASSIE'S COWBOY
by Diane Pershing (on sale April 2002)

A legacy of love arrives
BECAUSE OF THE RING
by Stella Bagwell (on sale May 2002)

*Available at
your favorite retail outlet.*

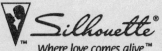

Where love comes alive™

Every day is

A Mother's Day

in this heartwarming anthology
celebrating motherhood and romance!

Featuring the classic story "Nobody's Child" by Emilie Richards
He had come to a child's rescue, and now Officer Farrell Riley was
suddenly sharing parenthood with beautiful Gemma Hancock.
But would their ready-made family last forever?

Plus two brand-new romances:

"Baby on the Way" by Marie Ferrarella
Single and pregnant, Madeline Reed found the perfect husband in the
handsome cop who helped bring her infant son into the world. But did his
dutiful role in the surprise delivery make J. T. Walker a daddy?

"A Daddy for Her Daughters" by Elizabeth Bevarly
When confronted with spirited Naomi Carmichael and her brood of girls,
bachelor Sloan Sullivan realized he had a lot to learn about women!
Especially if he hoped to win this sexy single mom's heart....

Available this April from Silhouette Books!

Where love comes alive™

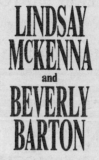